ZERO SUM GAME

A SID RUBIN SILICON ALLEY ADVENTURE

STEFANI DEOUL

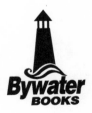

Bywater
BOOKS

Ann Arbor
2018

Bywater Books

Print ISBN: 978-1-61294-141-7

Bywater Books First Edition: December 2018

Printed in the United States of America on acid-free paper.

Cover designer: Ann McMan, TreeHouse Studio

Bywater Books
PO Box 3671
Ann Arbor MI 48106-3671
www.bywaterbooks.com

To: 14

Love: 16

"Each friend represents a world in us,
a world possibly not born until they arrive,
and it is only by this meeting that a new world is born."

—Anais Nin

PROLOGUE

"I know something you don't know."

I freeze mid-sentence, stare across the table at Imani, and deliberately avoid looking up at the encroaching singsong taunt-er, knowing full well I am the taunt-ee. You would think by now this would be an old routine for him, but apparently not. Thus, I force my eyes to remain staring straight ahead and reply, "Not possible," using my flattest-affect voice.

"Nope, it's true." Jimmy takes a minute to smug up, then slides into the booth, kisses Imani hello, and turns back to me, where I am now rolling my eyes across the table. "There is a new Sherlock. One that I have watched and you," Jimmy pauses, takes a big theatrical sigh, which he follows by grabbing a handful of my fries and stuffing them in his mouth, before finally finishing, "have not."

I stare at him, trying to decide how I am supposed to answer this quasi-dare. Do I want to be disdainful? Do I want to disregard? I mull my choices, biting the inside of my lip.

The problem, my friends, is I know The Flynn too well. He knows something. Actually he knows two somethings. The first something is, he knows I love Sherlock.

And I mean, I love Sherlock: Sherlock, Watson, Moriarty, Sir Arthur Conan Doyle. You name it. I have my phone ring set to what I think is most likely a group of French horns because it feels so very *Hound of the Baskervilles*. It is also

1

why I insist on using Baskerville as my default font rather than, oh, Arial or Times Roman or even some random impossible-to-read party font.

And my love is all encompassing, up to and including the Benedict Cumberbatch adaptation. Honestly, I did not think anything would come close to the Robert Downey Jr./Jude Law version. Which is such an amazing feast of steampunk deliciousness, a buffet of gorgeous frame after gorgeous frame. And we all know how I feel about my punking-of-the-steam.

Pause for a hand over heart moment.

And you know, just to share an icing-on-the-cake tidbit (buffet cake, get it?) a woman designed that one. Sarah Greenwood. Which really makes me happy. And envious. And off topic.

On topic, we can discuss the Jonny Lee Miller/Lucy Liu version. While it might not be my personal fav, come on, Lucy Liu as Watson? Whoa. We are talking serious eyeball ease. Of course we can also go old school and there's Basil Rathbone, Jeremy Brett, Peter Cushing, and even Vasily Livanov.

Yeah, I know, if I've reached Vasily Livanov, I may as well concede. I have to know what The Flynn knows. I give a slight head bob.

"Well, well, well, Ms. J-Pop, K-Pop, C-Pop." Jimmy smiles. Closed mouth, a bit patronizing. He takes a minute, stretches his arms out in front of him, fingers linked, and cracks his knuckles.

This is going to be painful.

"So I got home late from practice last night, and there's Mom sitting on the couch, watching some TV. Well, wouldn't you know, she motions me over to come sit with her while I eat. Needless to say, I was not thrilled."

Quick pause to explain: Jimmy's mom is Japanese-American, born in Charleston to Japanese immigrant parents. In order to maintain her fluency, she watches

2

Japanese movies and shows, and she raised Jimmy on them, so he would learn the language. When we were little kids, he had to go to Japanese class, but then he became a star quarterback, and that was one of the things that went away. I had to go to Hebrew school, but since I didn't become a star quarterback, it didn't go away. At least not until after the bat mitzvah. Just sayin'.

But anyway, his mom still tries.

"And then," Jimmy leans back, which I know means he is finally closing in on his point, "as I'm watching I realize Mom is actually watching Sherlock Holmes. Only," Jimmy pauses, looks at me and then turns conspiratorially to Imani, and continues his dramatic aside *sotto voce*, as though I am not there. "This Sherlock doesn't look like that Sherlock. How confounding. And it occurs to me, Sid Rubin shockingly does not know about this. Why?" And turning back to me, his smugness concludes, "Because she hasn't rambled on about it," pause for effect, "endlessly."

By now I am glaring at him, stalling, while trying to read my racing mind. And then I have it! He was watching Japan's *Miss Sherlock* with Yuko Takeuchi and Shihori Kanjiya. Duh!

Wowzerhole, he's right. And wrong. Wrong because I do know about it. Right because I forgot to track it down and become obsessed. I am going to blame our rather recent bout of LARPing for this lapse. Hey, it's a lot of work chasing a killer through a live action role-playing game!

However, before I can decide how I am going to toss my retort, all of our phones ping at once. It's Ari.

Vik. Melting down. Something about his stuff being gone. He's pissed. Presentation in two hours, needs to get ready, not listening. Need help.

And with that, Sherlock will have to wait.

We scramble to collect our stuff and head out when it occurs to me that, for the second time in one conversation, my spectacular wit and winning logology have failed me.

I should have proclaimed, "The game's afoot." It was so easy.

And I missed it.

It's official. My brain has oxidized. My rust is showing.

ONE

Rust?

Yes, rust. As in, impaired by neglect. Not to be confused with the video game version. Although, come to think of it, since that *Rust* has only one aim, to survive at all costs, it might also fit our bill, which in fairness might seem a bit melodramatic, but we are teenagers, we're entitled.

And confinement will do this to you.

Yes, confinement.

We, as in me, Sidonie "Sid" Rubin, geek lesbionic brainiac, along with my best bud forever, star quarterback, future Supreme Court Justice, Jimmy aka "Five Fingers" Flynn and his new girlfriend, the aforementioned Imani Cruz, who you might remember, before she started dating Jimmy was my other best friend from the day we met (yes, still not quite fully adjusted)—we are nearly, but not quite, right where you left us.

I say not quite, because if we were actually right where you left us, we would be indulging our latte cravings at our favorite haunt, the attitudinally challenged Perk This—an environment that somehow makes Imani's inability to grasp even the most basic math kind of charming.

But sadly we are not there, and there is no charm here.

Here, as in stuck, trapped, slowly suffocating, choking in the soul-sucking, cinderblock, spirit-bannered school lunch hall, suffering from complications caused by serious latte withdrawal, and lack of any other senior-year-of-high-school urban creature comfort. A harsh reality we are forced to endure because our parents, both singularly and collectively, have yet to express anything other than disbelief and anger since our "ill-conceived" (their word, not mine) late-night LARPing-to-find-a-killer expedition. Apparently neither the intent, nor the ultimate success behind our actions, warrants redemption.

Okay. Fair enough. Forget redemption. How about sympathy, or empathy? Compassion maybe. Or even pity? I'm not proud; I will take pity.

Nothing. Nada. Zero. Zilch. I have to say, I'm kind of disappointed in them.

And for the record, we did not embrace our fate quietly. *Au contraire, mes amis.*

Our first attempt to outthink our restrictions and avoid the complete humiliation of being a senior spotted in the lunchroom involved subverting said restrictions by high-jacking the sofas in the back of Mr. Clifton's Adventures in Morality, Legality, and Life classroom as our private cafe. But shockingly, and even worse sadly, the heretofore, ultra-cool, motorcycle-riding Mr. Clifton was not interested in being perceived as supporting our foray into sleuthing and other suddenly "anarchistic activities."

Yeah, that's the one I didn't see coming.

I don't know; maybe it was the gunfire.

Which puts us here, kicked back to the low-ceilinged lunch hall of backless hard benches and horrendous fluorescent lighting, when for a brief moment there was a shimmer of light, and it looked as though, yet again, we had discovered another loophole allowing us to circumvent the worst of it all.

Because if we think our public shaming isn't bad enough, forcing us to actually eat the school lunches is even worse (although I will confess to a weird fascination with, bordering on fondness for, those English Muffin Pizza-with-American-Cheese things). And it is worse-ness compounded, if you consider the world's greatest food is mere steps away from the main entrance, close enough to inhale, and yet we cannot leave school grounds to go get it.

But I did say we found a loophole—or at least we thought we did.

Ari, the ever-flirtatious, larger-than-life Arianna Wilson, actually can go outside, because her Mom is apparently way more chill, or at least way less interested, than the rest of ours.

And while once upon a time, Vikram might have escaped sharing our fate, being as he is the only son with five sisters in a fairly traditional family (translation: he tends to get away with murder), now his parents' joy that their son and Jimmy, the star quarterback, have somehow become friends seems to have ironically both raised and lowered his familial position.

As in, sadly for him, his fate is now irrevocably tied to ours.

A new reality he discovered at the LARP after-party, which was held in the hospital emergency room, where although I stressed I was fine, I was taken by ambulance to be "checked out."

That meeting, which sealed all our fates, did not disappoint. It was intense, equal parts bloody, merciless, and occasionally funny . . . if you happen to be a fan of gallows humor. It went down in the hospital corridor, right outside the glass window of my room, with the five of us trapped inside, huddling, hunkering and striving to be invisible, while the parental voices and gestures were like a tsunami, rising up and consuming the hallway.

According to Imani, this cacophony is exactly what it's like to sit in on a UN meeting gone wrong.

Led by my suddenly very French Maman, in full beautiful monster aka *bête belle* mode, with Dad trying to keep his anger in check just enough so that there will be some semblance of rational containment, the voices started off low and determined. We could distinctly hear Jimmy's Southern Japanese-American Mom's drawl grow broader as she vetted her ten ways to kill us now, while his Irish-Bostonian Dad was so angry that when he began ratcheting up the group vocal level, we honestly couldn't quite understand a word he was saying.

Vik's Mom, in the meantime, was gesticulating so wildly, her sunburnt-orange sari was like a tapestry "taken by the wind," while his Dad just kept up this kind of "no no no" headshake and tongue-clucking thing.

Then finally, as though they were a few minutes fashionably late to the party, enter Imani's Mom, beautiful, tall, very elegant and her Dad, impossibly taller and incredibly dashing. They came striding down the hallway looking exactly like they were TV casting for the Kenyan ambassador couple. And since Dr./Ms. Asha Cruz was in an unbelievably elegant, tapered dress, and Dr./Mr. Antonio Cruz was in an equally elegant tuxedo, modern enough that despite my impaired condition, I had a pang of wishing it was mine, it seemed a safe guess they came directly from some dignitary function.

And they were fierce. Picture a very suave, Afro-Latino James Bond and his incredibly bold, sexy date being called away from defending the crown because they are needed to, I don't know, referee a beer brawl. Yeah. They were most definitely not a happy twosome. Ow.

Although I have to say, Imani's Mom wears anger really well.

Yeah. Okay. In full confession mode here, I have been crushing on Imani's Mom since the day I met her. Which would be right when I turned twelve and was, let's just say, coming into my own. Mentally. Physically. *Hormonally.*

And Asha kind of looks like the model, Iman (which is why I swear they named Imani, Imani, although Imani totally denies it), and when she walks, it's like she's actually catwalking, or something. For a solid year every time I

8

would go over to Imani's house and her Mom would be around, I would go home and play a little David Bowie "it's like putting out the fire with gasoline"—on a loop. So when people need to ask, "what was my first clue . . ."

"God, she is so hot."

And the room turned to look at me.

Which is unfortunately how I realized I was apparently using my outside voice.

Oops.

Now if this was any form of a usual circumstance I would absolutely be mortified, but one, I was slightly injured and on drugs, and two, my crush on Imani's Mom is such old news as to be a yawn-fest, and three, almost as if she somehow heard me, Asha turned around and stared into the room, delivering us a message so loud and clear, any theoretical ribald remarks were instantly silenced as we all shrank down in an effort to somehow hide from our sealed fate.

Because if we thought their arrival might offer a potential diplomatic solution, we could all now rest uncomfortably assured we were wrong. Dr. Asha Cruz's scathing, taut, unblinking look guaranteed us they were not here as angels of mercy coming to our rescue. Nope. There would be no diplomatic aid, nor any kind of international bailout.

Which brought me back to our loophole.

We thought that, granted, while we would still be forced to sit and *eat* in the cafeteria, we could maintain our senior superiority, and perhaps even enhance it, or at least maybe flaunt it—just the tiniest bit—by allowing the masses to drool as we chowed down on food, gathered by Ari-the-reigning-queen-of-the-unfettered-by-parents, from the magnificent plethora of food trucks parked a mere one avenue away. Which is pretty darn close, because in New York City, avenue blocks are fairly short (it's the street blocks that are long). So it seemed a clever answer to our dire situation and honestly pretty easy-peasy.

But I ask you, is anything ever really easy-peasy?

By day three, Ari is whining that the bags are too heavy, the orders are too big, and she is losing way too much Vikram-the-boyfriend time. I will point out that Vikram's lunch is also in this run. But Ari gets a little irritable—okay, a lot irritable—and her bitchwhinemoan level increases until it becomes sharply deafening and thus we are once again forced to adjust.

So now she gets our lunch on Fridays, but the rest of the time, we are forced to suck it up and tray it with the underclass masses.

I do take some pride in never making eye contact with my younger brother, Jean (of the French pronunciation, "zhan," which no one uses because where would be the fun in that, "Yoo Hoo, Eu-*gene!*") Shallow, I know. And yes, he did come through when we needed him, but I still will not be seen lunching with him. Nope. Not going to happen. Cheap thrill. Small victory. Big Sigh.

And so ladies and gentlemen, and everyone else on the gender-fluid spectrum, we are now three weeks in, with no freedom in sight. Yep. Three weeks down, the rest of our senior year to go.

Today, Jimmy is off hanging out (or hiding out) somewhere, while you have come to find me sitting with Imani (of the stunning looks, massive language skills, and fantastic acting chops), knowing we are embarked on a nearly futile mission: getting Imani to understand the infamous mathematical word problem. An issue you may be quite familiar with. As in, you kind of either get them—or you don't. Sadly, Imani falls into the "don't" category.

So I sit here, alternating between drumming my pencil and miserably watching the jumbo second hand of the cafeteria clock tick, and indulging my masochistic self, dying over and over, in Hiro!!'s brilliant, evil, warped *Trap Adventure 2*, waiting discontentedly for Imani to have a miraculous breakthrough, or something else, anything else, to come into my life and make this moment somehow less wallowing. The ubiquitous "be careful what you wish for."

Right on cue, as if he heard my silent plea, enter stage left one Vikram Patel, toting one cheap beige cafeteria tray, scanning the room for our location.

And boom, we are spotted; let the beeline begin.

Watching Vikram hop, skip and zigzag his way closer, I am weirdly mesmerized by his approach. He is oddly, awkwardly bounding, attempting to battle through the maze of kids, circumventing all those pushed and strewn chairs, going left to get right. But as he is pausing here and there, he looks up and it's almost as if he is sniffing the air, finding us, and then grinning again.

And although I'm not sure I know why, as I watch him navigate this maze, I get "the hackles" and instantly know he is way too happy for my own good. And then, not only do I surprise myself by hearing my own suspicious, random *I think I liked you better when I thought you were a loser*, but simultaneously, almost as though it is an echo, except it isn't, from somewhere deep in the recesses of my mind, I also hear my mother's voice, replete with her withering sense of droll, *"Je dis qu'il y a anguille sous roche,"* which actually translates to, "I sense there is an eel under a rock." Or, to put it my way . . .

. . . I smell a rat.

TWO

But if Vikram is a rat caught in a maze, his twitching whiskers lead me to believe he has just found his cheese. I'm hoping, at the very least, we rate a good triple-crème brie.

Hey, it's important to me. I am French. Well, half French. But my palate is defiantly French when it comes to cheese.

And with one last twitch, Vik announces, "Okay, I've got it."

Vikram's pronouncement startles Imani, who has maintained blissful unawareness of his rather haphazard arrival by being intently focused on her unsolvable, unknowable arithmetic mess—which if you say it with third syllable emphasis, as in a-rith-MAT-tic, like aromatic, it gives it a nice flair.

"One word." Vikram plunks his tray down and lifts up his index finger, an apparent visual accompaniment for effect. "Robotics!"

Wow. Color me underwhelmed.

"No." Vikram slides onto the bench next to Imani and across from me. "I am telling you, this is a good thing. Trust me. Smitty's class."

Pause to explain. Smitty is Mr. Smithers, and he teaches an AP Physics C class. Everything one needs to know can be summed up in five words: there are only five students. Vikram is one.

And before we can actually get into his obviously

weighty and purposeful logic regarding robotics, we must first take a moment to notice a flouncing Ari and her tossing head, in which we might espy a new dark purple dye-block in her hair. We respond, on cue, with an appropriate ooh and ahh.

Entrance achieved, Ari nudges the crowded side of the bench over, so she can sit next to, or more accurately all over, Vikram. So even though I know Imani obviously has nothing to do with this, I'm suddenly feeling played in a game of three on one.

"Okay. Look. I have to take on the robotics challenge. It's part of Smitty's class every year. And to do it properly requires a team. And this year it's the twentieth anniversary for our school. So it's a really big deal. And I am thinking," his voice suddenly raises half an octave, moving into plea mode, "we should all be a part of the team."

I'm pretty sure my quirking eyebrow screams my unspoken rapid-fire questions, *We? What we? And why would we ever want to do that?* because Vikram quickly looks away from me, presumably in search of a less hostile eyebrow, and his speech gets even more rushed than usual.

"This way we all will be contributing on behalf of our school, which will make our teachers and our parents happy. And, they will need to let us get together to work on this, which will make me happy. And, it will be very helpful for college applications," Vikram moves to seal the deal, now glancing to me and then over to Imani, "and not just mine."

As much as I want to just go along and agree, something about this is bothering me. As the expression expresses, it's right there on the tip of my tongue.

Now if someone would just read it for me.

However, Ari is too busy congratulating her boyfriend on his pleading presentation, by reading his tongue with her tongue, to be available to read mine. Wow. Tongue and then some.

"Ewwww." This is way more than I need to see. "Get your tongues out of each other's mouths."

"Don't be ewwwing me, Missy."

While I am not wishing to be the target of Ari's attack, she thankfully must retract her tongue to turn toward me in order to tell me off. "If you hadn't needed all of us for your LARPing exhibition, I would be outside somewhere, not stuck in here, and I would be seeing my boyfriend, all of my boyfriend to be specific, and you would not be suffering seeing my tongue . . ." pause for liberal use of said tongue to make lascivious motions at me. ". . . in action."

Which in turn, causes me to blush and also rules out any ability I might have had to protest about how I don't remember twisting anyone's arm here. I really need to work on this whole blush thing.

"Hey!" Apparently my reading Ari's tongue is as good as getting someone to read what was on the tip of mine. Go figure. Because now I know exactly what was flitting about just out of reach.

"You said," my eyeballs turning to stare at Vikram, my finger pointing like a sideways loser sign, "you said part, part of a team." My suspicious mind is flying. "Who exactly is your team?"

Aha! Dead silence. Followed by suspiciously shifty eye movement. It would seem that as Ari released Vikram's tongue, the cat got it.

And the cat is hanging on really tight as Vikram and I now sit frozen in a silent stare-off.

But I will warn you, this cat is no freaking match for Sid the Huntress.

And thus, almost as though he knows he is being stalked by my fierceness, Vikram blinks. And then folds. And a confession whimpers out, "Mae Ann and Mae Lee."

"The Twincesses? You have the freaking Twincesses?!" I am horrified.

"Look." Having the lie of omission ripped from his lips has now caused his voice to rise a full octave and quaver slightly. "It doesn't really work that way. I mean for the beginning stages we kind of have two teams, but then we all have to work together and you know, I don't have a huge choice. Smitty made Marcus the other captain. So either I go for the Lau twins or I have to pick Hand Jive." Vikram raises his eyes back to me. "What would you do?"

Moi? What would I do? I would move to the Island of Themyscira. I would go directly to Queen Hippolyta and her sister, Antiope. I would throw myself at their mercy, pleading with them not to make me do this.

I would also—if I could somehow figure out an, ahem, lawful way to download the first twenty minutes of *Wonder Woman*, screenshot it and then tape it frame by frame on the wall of my bedroom so when I turn out the lights my night sky would glow down and transport me away—do that too.

But that's off topic, and sadly there is no Themyscira here.

I wonder if I were to reach out to my personal patron saint of comics, Gail Simone, with some kind of emergency beacon or secret-coded SOS, would she write me my own superhero way out of this? I mean I wouldn't need her to make me incredibly cool or anything, just a simple super-power to make really annoying classmates go away to a distant planet, in another galaxy, far, far from Earth, where they can happily live out their days, terrorizing themselves to their hearts' content.

Because I will give Vikram this much, his choices do suck. He is correct about that. Hand Jive Olney is Scott Olney. He got this last nickname in the fourth grade. It was a kind of a step up from his previous nickname, Jack-Off Olney.

As you can rightly assume, my friends, he was blessed

with such lasting descriptors because he couldn't stop playing with himself in class, which I do have to say caused the school—and our parents—to invest in a much earlier sex education moment than was probably comfortable.

And in fairness, Scott goes to therapy two or three days a week, still. And while he hasn't had any, let's just say, obvious flare-ups in at least five or six years, some nicknames never die. There's always at least one kid who can't resist. And in Hand Jive's case, with or without his compulsion, he's still the creepiest kid in the school, so it's probably never going to leave him.

So teaming him with Marcus is a good idea. Marcus Johnston is a really cool, super-chill dude. Much like Jimmy, he's the kind of guy everyone wants to say hi to. A huge, easy smile and an outsized, loose-curl afro that every girl—yes, people, including me—just wants to play with. He is almost enough to make even me rethink my lesbionic classification and declare myself . . . Pause for just a second. He is almost enough to make me think, exception to rule. No. That's not it either. You know what, I'm just going to say, Marcus is almost enough. But still, not quite.

But to Vikram's point, in spite of having Hand Jive in tow, Marcus will have no issue finding willing minions to join his team.

Which brings us back to Vikram and the Twincesses. I believe we're supposed to feel sorry for the Twincesses. The story is their dad moved here from China for some big job when their mom was pregnant. Their mom died in some accident or something when they were babies. So their grandmother, their mother's mother, moved from China to New York to take care of them. And if you think Tiger Moms—you know, the kind of mothers whose kids only get to participate if there's some kind of award to be won—are scary people, they are nothing next to a Tiger Grandma of motherless twin baby girls.

And all that might be okay, except now they're seventeen

and they still dress in identical, albeit incredibly expensive, designer outfits, which is really bizarre because they are fraternal twins who look nothing alike, other than they both look ridiculous. And they do everything together. Just the two of them.

They even have their own "secret language." And when they deign to actually speak to any of us, they have this affected Chinese accent thing they do—even though they have never lived in China. It's "lah" this and "lah" that. And as I said, they were born here. It's this whole weird twisted Twincess thing. And their number one rule, as if you couldn't guess, is *they* are always perfect and *you* are always not perfect.

So to state the obvious, I really, really can't stand them.

Which means I know I should absquatulate. Vamoose. Make like a banana and split.

But before thought can turn to motion, Imani, yes, my bestie (!) turns back to Vikram and states, "Ignore her."

Which she follows by motioning Vik to come close. She proceeds to then drop her voice into one of those dramatic "asides" she learned. You know, where she's "whispering" but you can still hear her all the way in the back of the theater, effectively making her target, Vikram, her confidant, all while ensuring everyone, especially me, can still hear her loud and clear. "She's still suffering from the PAPEs." And as Imani pronounces this, her head whips back at me and does that tilt-y kind of peer-me-down thing.

I respond by bugging my eyes at her and swinging my left hand, open palm, forward. A silent tableau of gesture, screaming, *What?*

"PAPE. As in Post Adrenaline-Post Emma syndrome." Her pause is apparently for added smugness. "I made it up. Even gave it a catchy acronym 'cause I know how much you like that kind of thing."

This time Imani's pause is long enough to let the words sink in and toss me a fake smile and change the pitch of her voice. "It's been going on for weeks. And you know what, Sid, it's gotten pretty damn tiresome."

Wow. Shade thrown straight to the bull's-eye.

And before I can work up to personal indignation, Ari leans into the table, pushing Vik back, coming nearly across, and then turning to Imani, "I guess that's to be expected when before your crush can break your heart," pause for a calculated shrug, "you just break your crush."

And with that, Ari turns her self-satisfied smirk to me, and holds up her right hand, so Imani can high-five it, right on cue.

I sit up, lean forward and then slink back. I want to defend my honor and dispute this besmirchment, but I can't. I think Imani's PAPE diagnosis is pretty low-blow, but it is arguably accurate. Meeting Detective Emma Macdonald, the live-action version of my entire teenage fantasy crush, and having her be definitively, unquestionably unavailable was a cataclysmic blow. Even if a person could argue the fantasy might have been a bit ridiculous to begin with. It was still *my* fantasy. And nowhere in that fantasy did leaping from a balcony and landing on her pelvis and shattering it play out.

Not to mention catching a serial killer while having my friends shot at while throwing myself off said ledge, culminating in being gulaged by my parents, I will admit, maybe has resulted in a bit of post-something petulance. But I think I'm entitled.

And I don't think she needed to acronym it.

That's kind of harsh.

I am wounded.

But even my newly crafted boo-boo face is for naught. I get nothing. Not an inch, not a flinch. It seems her mercy meter has overloaded and now, done with me, Imani turns back to Vik, who at least has the decency to look shocked, as opposed to, I don't know, let's say his girlfriend, Ari, who is laughing hysterically and actually putting her hand up for a high-five. And as Imani makes contact, Ari asks, "So how exactly does this robot thing work?"

PALM. FOREHEAD. KABOOM!

And just like that, we are all in.

THREE

I don't know, I still feel very *Hunger Games* nominated.

But who knows, maybe I am being overly pessimistic, even perhaps . . . wrong. I know, shocking. However, let us not forget, I was recently diagnosed as suffering from a severe case of the PAPEs.

And, you know, maybe robotics actually won't be so bad. Vikram cut a deal with Marcus saying if he got me to agree to code for them and Jimmy to agree to drive (because he does happen to have the best hand-eye coordination in the school) Marcus will keep the Lau twins on his roster through the first section. Then, we'd most likely be on different committees anyway.

So bad might even turn ever so slightly good as, more importantly, Vikram turned out to be right. Well, not about isolating the Lau twins. That jury is still out.

But yes. He was right that the logjam, the stalemate—the utter torture that comes from jailers and jail-ees knowing they have maxed their punishment and amends quotients but not knowing how to graciously acknowledge this and move forward—is finally broken.

Vikram's class project allows all parental units to feel virtuous as our reins are relinquished, our tethers gathered in, and we are freed. We have been chastised, they are vindicated, and we all move along.

Happy dance time!

Or not.

It all starts innocently enough. Imani and I are feeling pretty darn good, two-stepping our way down to Perk This. Down the school steps we fly, out the front gates. Breathing deeply. Old familiar smells. Swerving right, dancing left. Old familiar sights. Dodge the never-ending scaffolding two blocks down. Old familiar sewer grates. This is our hood and it is perfect.

Rounding the final corner, four stores down, we arrive and pause for just a minute, standing in front, looking at the signage, drinking it all in (pun intended), just grinning.

I step up, swing the door open, bow, and with a flourish, "After you m'lady." Imani curtsies and with a backward sweep of her hand and a "why thank you" she disappears inside. I follow directly behind and, whoa, body-slam right into her. Which, if this was a different story, might have been a very interesting portent of cheap thrills. But there is no playfulness in this tale. Only woefulness.

You see, Imani and I have had dibs on the same couches forever. I mean for four years of high school we've been spending more or less every day here after classes, except for the days she has play rehearsals, or a show, or the odd moment when I actually have a life. So, that corner setup, it's kind of ours.

At least it was. Until today.

Today there is a group of six kids of the unknown variety using our couch-table-side chair setup. And there's nothing we can do. I mean, I can think of ten things I *want* to do, starting with going over and saying, "save-ies" like I'm four years old, but I can't. Not that it would have done me any good even when I was four, but this is just wrong.

That is our space.

Or at least, it was. Our space.

So instead of rushing to order our lattés and muffins, we're kind of just standing here, maybe two feet inside the door, staring, completely lost about what comes next. And it's a weird sensation. Maybe we're experiencing what people call a sobering moment. And it sucks.

I suddenly realize, staring at this group of usurpers, between getting grounded and Imani and Jimmy's busy dating schedule (which because we are grounded and it's still football season is incredibly erratic), how long it has been since we, me and Imani, just sat and hung out for a latté or two.

Once we would have laughed and done something really obnoxious like sitting on the back edge of the couch, laughing and singing annoying show tunes until the interlopers finally got it and gave up "our table."

I remember one time there were some would-be interlopers and it took us, I think, until the third chorus of "It's the Hard-Knock Life" from *Annie* for us to finally get to them. (For the record, I do believe Imani has played every orphan up to, and including, Annie. I will be hearing "the sun will come out tomorrow" forever and ever and ever . . . and ever. Yes, I am a very good friend.) Hard to say. Good times.

But standing here, we see them laughing, computer wires everywhere fighting over the one lonely, precious outlet, and I realize we have kind of grown too distant to own that space. And I don't mean too distant from each other. That won't ever happen. It's just too distant like too long gone. From here. And I feel my eyes tear up. We are standing here, bearing witness to our own *petite mort*, small death. It hurts.

But then my ear tickles and I hear very quietly, "We are so much cooler than they can even dream of being." Imani reaches back, takes my hand, and gives it a squeeze.

And with that, the personal pity party spell is broken.

It takes me a minute to get the eye-welling to recede, but I squeeze back. And then, then I've got it. I shift, grab my phone, text and hit send. I clamp onto Imani's hand, pulling her out the door.

"Where are we going?"

I pause mid-tug so I can focus on her. "*Our* place."

It takes a moment for her to get it. Her smile becomes huge, and I wait for it, and she doesn't disappoint as her full-throated laugh comes flying out. And as if on cue, a sweep of wind lifts her amazing curls so they can provide a perfect snapshot. And god, she, Imani Cruz, is so freaking beautiful. And she's my friend.

And all of a sudden I realize I'm happy she's dating Jimmy. That I'm really happy Imani's happy, and that I love her and I've missed her so much.

Imani is right. I had let the Post Adrenaline-Post Emma syndrome consume me. So I inhale deep and release the PAPE to the atmosphere. I busticate it so bad, it is in smithereens!

PAPE BE GONE.

I lean over, kiss her cheek, grab her hand and we take off laughing, running down the street. And it is so cheesy, so totally cornball, but suddenly the two of us are singing, "if you're happy and you know it clap your hands."

And mind you, not that I actually remember, but I'm pretty sure it's Imani who completely starts this inanity.

It's absurd and silly and we nearly run over this one lady, who must be at least one hundred and ninety years old, pushing one of those wire carts people use to go to the market. And you know, she is seriously tiny. Like, barely bigger than her cart tiny. All shriveled and wrinkled and we must have been laughing so hard at each other, because by the time we see her, it is too late to stop.

But she had seen us. And she huddles there frozen, terrified, as we come towering, thrusting down upon her.

I don't know how, but we somehow manage to get our hands up and over, making way for her hunched body to pass safely "under London Bridge." Immediately we twirl back to her and just stand there. It takes a minute, even though it feels like forever, but then looking at the two of us stopped with our chagrined, scrunched faces, she slowly turns her fear into a tentative smile until she, too, manages a small laugh.

Released from our fear and shame, Imani blows the lady a kiss, grabs my hand, and once again we take off. Quietly advancing up to the corner, turning right and losing it. We're now both laughing and weeping, the insane laughter of those who have cheated certain death.

"Oh my god, Sid," says Imani, who finally chokes out a couple of words. "This is so" *gasp* "not funny." *Gasp. Gasp.* "We could have killed her."

And just as I am trying to take this in and sober up, she finishes her thought.

"I mean, did you see her face?" And actress that she is, Imani strikes a ridiculous pose, and that's all it takes for us both to lose it again.

Which means, fifteen minutes later we are still here, because every time one of us starts to get it under control, we look at the other one and another fit of hyperventilation begins.

And by now, we can't stop and it hurts. Really bad. The stitch in my side is now a stab. Doubled over. Can't breathe. Sucking wind. I slump against the brick wall and lower myself to the ground. Heaving. Panting. Imani has her back to me and is using her arms to brace against the wall and has crossed her very tense, very straight legs. Ooh. I'm thinking that's, wow, not good.

But somehow we do finally run out of gas and slowly head back out, still avoiding direct eye contact while gingerly rebuilding a bit of our mojo over the last few blocks.

Until right on our very late cue, we happily stomp our feet at the front door of Platitudes, push it open and see our grumpy waitress whose name I never did find out. She honestly doesn't seem as happy to see me as I am to see her, but I wave and we continue on, playfully making our way to the back, where we are apparently the first to arrive.

In anticipation, we get waters all the way around. And here, my friends, is where we began. Jimmy saunters in, begins Sherlock-taunting me, when our phones ping. It's Ari. Vikram is freaking out, and we are on the move. Racing back out the door, I do actually think this isn't going to help make our waitress happy to see us.

FOUR

Down the steps to the subway, we are off to Jackson Heights, which is no mere hop, skip, and jump. But miraculously we manage to grab an express, which gets us there in decent time, race back up the steps, and unexpectedly run right into Ari pacing up and down, obviously agitated and nervous, waiting for us.

"I can't go to his apartment alone." Ari launches right into it. "His family is super traditional. There's no way his mother is letting some girl go up to his room. And he's stopped answering me when I text."

"I get that." Jimmy wraps Ari in a hug. "Do you know what happened?"

"Not all of it. Vik was supposed to meet Marcus after lunch today to go over their robotics presentation. And he texted Marcus to say he'd left his notes back home, and was Marcus cool if they met at four instead. Marcus said fine. Vik went home. And then, I'm not sure, but I think when he was on the train, he logged onto *Contagion*, and I don't know, something about he's been hacked."

Okay, quick aside. You need to know that when Vikram has any spare time, he plays the online game *Contagion*, and he's done it pretty much forever. *Contagion* is what is classified as an MMORPG, a massive multiplayer online role-playing game.

Which, for the uninitiated, is a video game that takes place in what's called a persistent state world (PSW) where

26

thousands or millions of players create their own character to participate in whatever the game they're playing demands. So in the case of *Contagion*, theoretically someone is collecting enough loot, maybe a stash of various antibiotics, safe harbors, or whatever, to escape the increasingly deadly outbreaks.

If you're someone who's actually never played an MMORPG, the most addicting thing is that the virtual world is always changing. So whenever you log off, other events are continuously unfolding across *Contagion* that may affect you whenever you log on again.

And as I said, Vikram's been at it forever. And I mean forever. Like, since the day it launched. And Vik's really good, like, he was ranking-number-seven-on-the-planet-or-something, good. Which means he's amassed a huge amount of really powerful stuff. And while dating Ari caused his ranking to slip a bit, our parental incarceration gave him plenty of time to rebuild his status.

By now we are walking, and as Ari talks I am hearing her, but attempting to ogle Jackson Heights. I have been here a few times, but not much. It's actually in Queens, kind of at Seventy-Fourth Street between Roosevelt Avenue and Thirty-Seventh Avenue. And as we are walking, there's Bollywood and Bhangra playing everywhere, and spices, wow, tons of spices and aromas.

Ari's fast pace is minimizing my view, but when we get caught waiting for traffic, I look to my left and see the best of it all. Right alongside us are tons and tons of shops showcasing colorful sari after sari, each one more striking than the next. Well, except for that turquoise-y peacock thing. That one's just bad.

Something about the whole eye-catching display makes me think of pictures I've seen of the Festival of Chalk, this giant spring festival, celebrated during *Holi*, where everyone goes into the streets and splatters everyone with dye and chalk. It looks like the most awesome time ever.

I never thought about it, but now I wonder if they cele-
brate it here? I mean, if they do, I could go this year. Of
course that won't be quite the same, but it would be way
cheaper and we could all go together. How amazing would
that be?

"Sid!"

Imani's scream interrupts what is my apparent daydream.
I dodge traffic, cross against the light, and catch back up to
the group, which by now is already nearly a block ahead.
We turn right, head another block over, and we are here.

We let Jimmy buzz and take the lead.

"Hi. Mrs. Patel. It's Jimmy, and Imani, and Sid, and Ari."
Jimmy checks each of us off, but keeps his finger on the
intercom. "Um, we were wondering if Vikram is here?"

And with the buzz back, we are in.

Third floor, to the left, down two more doors. I get the
feeling we are being followed. A feeling reasonably confirmed as Mrs. Patel opens the door before we can even
knock. Inside we find several of Vikram's "aunties" having tea.

Jimmy pardons our interruption, we all give little nods
and smiles before disappearing down the hall in the direction we are pointed.

Of course, as I have never been here before, I am checking
out every detail, so when we get down toward Vik's room, I
smile. Right across the hall I spy a conveniently open door,
which not only provides opportunity for me to peek in, it
seemingly commands me to do so. I check out what is obviously his sisters' room. In fairness, let me acknowledge it's a
pretty big room. Or at least it was. Until it had five beds and
dressers crammed into it! Whoa.

Before I begin fixating on how much I would hate that,
Imani nudges me. Jimmy is turned back, giving Mrs. Patel
a smile and a small wave of thanks as he is opening Vik's
door, which allows me a direct view of what must be the
perks of only "son-dom." Yes, it is a smaller room, but it's
Vik's alone.

So, of course, now I'm kind of knee-jerk annoyed. I mean, really? Couldn't they at least halve this or something? My feminist sensibilities are appalled. So are my encroachment challenges. Having less fun now.

Ari, in the meantime, is having plenty of fun, and is busy, let's just say . . . comforting . . . Vik, who is still sitting in his desk chair.

She is a very explicit comforter, you know.

I take advantage of Vikram's sudden inability to move his head left or right, to check out his screen. Even from my position hovering near the door, I have an unimpeded view, confirming Ari's interpretation of events is sadly right . . . and cringeworthy. So I do. Cringe. And wince. Vik's been wiped out.

During which time Imani steps in to take control of the scene, which is good. Someone has to. "Okay Vik, tell us what happened."

"I was coming home to grab some papers for tonight." Vikram wheels the chair around until it is more or less facing us. His voice is very low. I'm not sure if it's because he is so upset, or just so his mother won't hear us, but I sit down on the edge of his bed and lean in. Imani joins me there, as well. "I missed the express, so I thought I would just play a bit while I endured the freaking forever ride. I launch, check the leaderboard and there I am, still in the top ten, but my inventory is empty. Not one fucking thing. My entire inventory—gone. It's a complete wipeout. No weapons, no potions, no antidotes, no nothing."

Wow. So regardless of his ranking, he's been effectively neutered, rendered a zero. It's like gamer death, but with no honor. Or maybe it's really a case of gamer murder. Who stole everything and left him here to die?

And he stares at us all, monotonously answering our obvious and lame suggestions. Yes, he's not a frigging moron; yes, he tried rebooting. And yes, he's sent the makers a note. And yes and yes and yes.

For a minute, when he first began, with his very low voice, I thought he was exhausted, maybe even on the verge of tears. But I was wrong. Vikram isn't crying. Vikram Patel is furious, and he is so furious, he can barely speak. And when he does, it's a swear-infested frenzy.

I do realize everyone has bad moods and off days and all that kind of thing, especially teens, because as *everyone* knows adolescents are moody. It's written up in all the big studies. But none of us adolescents have ever seen Vikram angry. Not even Ari, who we all know has seen way more of Vikram than any of us even care to.

I look at him, I look at the screen, and it's all wrong. Incredibly wrong. But not something that can be righted right now. Right now Vik has a robotics challenge to reveal, and we need to get him out of here and over to the school before his day gets even worse.

FIVE

Which we do accomplish. Well, more or less. Although I think we can acknowledge Jimmy does the accomplishing more or less. He's really good with that whole "come from behind" huddle-speak. And truthfully, even with that, it's still more less than more. But we do get Vik's streaming invective-tude shut down long enough to get him past his Mom, the aunties, and the suddenly "suspect" watchful and reporting neighbors.

I am particularly not trusting the old lady sitting on the couch in the lobby with the hookah pipe. Imani disagrees, says she would be too obvious. I don't know, she is definitely creeping me out.

What it is about me and old ladies today?

But now is not the time for introspection. We need to get Vikram calm enough to talk, preferably without the spitting of vile epithets, catch the train, race back to school and pile into the auditorium. We do this with some serious aplomb, as though we suddenly used a turbo boost to vault our way right past the Goombas (of the *Super Mario* variety) and somehow we land squarely in the midst of the cool kids club . . .

. . . as in two cheerleaders front and center, along with nearly half the booster club.

Wowzerhole. Color me gawk-ed.

Marcus must have managed to sweet-talk them into showing up. Although, head swivel, over there, coming up on the right, is Jimmy's tight end Trey, along with a bunch of his o-line.

Vik veers off to join Marcus setting up. Ari pauses to watch him, while I pause to watch the Jimmy/Trey male fist bumping, chest bumping, and testosterone calling, "hey duding" all the way around. Which leads me to think maybe the cheerleaders actually do belong to Jimmy. Which, by extension, would put them on Vikram's count. Which would actually give Vikram Patel a cool count. Wow, pause to ingest that thought.

Of course, one would have to be counting.

Which of course, duh, I am. I mean, hello? We are talking about *moi*. I can tally this like nobody's business. It's a gift. Or at least a skill set learned sitting on the sidelines of grade school, lunchtime "throne of The Flynn" worshippers.

My running tally of impressiveness is surprisingly beginning to fully inoculate me against any hidden pessimistic, post-PAPE germs about this venture, which we do know could be silently circulating in my system, waiting to contage and force a relapse, when I espy one additional, and heretofore unaccounted for, hellish hiccup. It approaches with its traditional chin thrust.

"Ari, darling," she over-purrs, her pseudo-socialite trilling—or trolling, either works—out in full force.

Could someone explain to me how Janelle talks leading with her chin? It doesn't seem anatomically possible. "You were so right," pause for the hand-over-heart, shoulder-shrug, "everybody's here."

Improbable but apparently true, it seems Ari went and actually convinced Janelle, the official mouthpiece of our America, to show. Before I can even process running and hiding, the demon child turns to me. "And Sid, I'm ever so happy to see you've finally been set free."

I try to grunt something resembling an appropriate grunt.

I will share with you, my only upside to being grounded was "sadly being forced" to decline an invitation to Janelle's

32

stoplight party. You know, the kind of party where you "wear red if you're taken," "yellow if it's complicated," and "green," yes, you've guessed it, "if you're single and ready to mingle." Ick. Ick. Ick. Blech. I cannot think of anything I would rather do less.

Not even being grounded and playing endless board games with the parents.

Which actually wasn't too terrible, and sometimes even fun, and always way better than a stoplight party. Which is about the stupidest kind of party ever. I mean who is Janelle going to invite who doesn't already know I'm not seeing anyone? And if I was seeing someone secretly, it's not like I would be dumb enough to show up wearing red. Yuck. Even thinking of it now makes my eye twitch.

And everything Janelle is, and does, is all about the gossip. If she says hello in the hallways, you know you are now marked as prey. And if she nets you, you are now a meal she will regurgitate later, at oddly beneficial-to-her moments.

So to say I'm just not thrilling about seeing Janelle would be a massive understatement. But when I look over to Ari, she wrinkles her nose and shrugs. "You know, Sid, it's always better to keep her in tow than to let her roam the school unsupervised."

Before I can best decide how I would like to disagree vehemently with that, thankfully, or maybe mercifully for us all, a mic shriek intervenes, followed by the unmistakable *thump thump* noise of mic testing, followed by "Hello?"

The disembodied boom is coming from Marcus, who along with Vikram, has taken up position at the front of the auditorium, floor level in front of the stage. They have set up a table with a big-screen monitor, hooked into what must be Marcus's laptop.

"Okay. Now if everyone can just grab a seat down here somewhere . . ." And as we are all congregated at the top of the aisle, Marcus waits for us to come down, climb in, and get settled.

"So first, I want to welcome everyone to Cooper School's Team Thorium, and thank you for joining us as we enter this year's robotics competition. For those who don't know me, I am Marcus Johnston." Marcus pauses, casually letting his smile light up the room as the catcalls interrupt his opening. He takes a step back, puts his right hand up to his heart, giving two pats.

God. Is there anyone who can flirt better than Marcus?

Then with a wink to his fan base, he steps back up and leans in to continue. "I am the co-captain of this year's challenge, a position I share with our fellow classmate, Vikram Patel, and I have to say, as we stand here, we are feeling your love and we are loving your energy."

And as the saying goes, the crowd goes wild. We all cheer, and the applause, thankfully, does seem to give Vikram a still way-needed boost, as he smiles back to the crowd.

"You know," Marcus leans in, inviting us to conspire with his next thought, "they call *FIRST* POWER UP the ultimate Sport for the Mind, but for me and my pal, Vik, we would just like to say welcome to the hardest fun you'll ever have." As he glances about, Marcus catches Jimmy's eye and playfully wags his finger. "Even you, Mr. Five Fingers."

To which Jimmy blows an air kiss.

Before he loses control of the now-playfully hooting, revved-up crowd, Marcus holds up his left hand, motioning for quiet. "And this year that's doubly true. Because this year it's a special time to be a Thorium. It's the twentieth anniversary of our very first journey into competition, a competition in which the Thoriums brought home the Regional Rookie All-Star Award. Which was more than amazing. It was shocking and it was great." Marcus takes a brief pause, allowing a moment of reverence before continuing.

"But, my friends, a rookie all-star award won twenty years ago is not enough." Marcus's voice takes on power as he begins to preach from his pulpit. "Thoriums"—his hands grasp the podium, rocking it just a tiny bit—"Thoriums descend from Thor, the Norse God of Thunder *and* an Avenger. And with its atomic number of 90, Thorium is an elemental heavyweight. So this year, on our twentieth anniversary of competition, it is both a Thorium legacy— and a Thorium destiny—that together, together we will go all the way."

Marcus-the-rock-star pumps a fist and steps back, clearing the way for Vikram to take the podium.

Now, on a good day, Vikram's style might be described as a little deer-in-headlights. And today, as we all know, isn't a good day.

I can feel the four of us collectively tense as Vikram lurches forward.

As he looks up, I suck in my reaction before it can escape. All Vik's rage from earlier is gone, and it's as if he's joined the undead. And this undead-blob-of-walking-misery thing apparently not only drains all the color from your skin, but it crushes your vocal chords, causing your voice to go completely flat, and leaving you devoid of life. Wow.

Maybe we should have left him seething.

"So, I too, thank you for coming. Before I read our mission statement, let's all give a round of applause to Mr. Smithers, better known to all of us as Smitty."

Vikram never looks up, never makes eye contact, as he reads from his notes. "Because even though it is a class assignment for us, it is also one for him. Smitty is our first mentor on this ride, and his commitment to us is to match our commitment."

The clapping is not a deafening roar.

Ah, Vik, you are so killing it. And not in a good way.

However, before the air is completely sucked out of the room, leaving us to suffocate and die, Marcus spins in, wrapping Vikram up in one of those left-armed buddy hugs. "Come on people, let's give it up for the Smit-man!"

And right on cue, everyone applauds Smitty, who has positioned himself somewhere in the back of the room, which would make this a likely moment to get some first-rate neck-craning time. Except I don't. Because I can't stop staring at Vikram, who stands there, looking miserable, like a wet, ratty dog who so does not like the rain.

As the applause stops, Vikram musters himself back up, all the way to zombie, and continues. "Our goal is to bring together mentors, engineers and students through an engineering and robotics challenge. We will learn by using the latest technology infused with positive attitudes."

Positive attitude. Wow, there's bitter irony for you. Big Sigh. Poor Vik.

"We will succeed by committing acts of gracious professionalism on and off the playing field."

Gracious professionalism. Now that has a nice ring. Or it would . . . if it was delivered by a breathing person.

"Mouthful, huh?" Marcus thrusts his energetic presentation-saving self back to front and center. "The single most important element to our success, *Gracious Professionalism*, is an ideology defined by Dr. Woodie Flowers. And in his defining concept, fierce competition and mutual gain are not separate notions. Gracious professionals learn and compete like crazy, but treat one another with respect and kindness in the process." And then, a small pause, before finishing with what sounds like a small warning, "They avoid treating anyone like losers."

As Marcus talks, my eyes roam the room until they land on the Twincesses, only to find Twincess A, Mae Ann, staring back at me. Her fingers lift up from her lap just enough to make a small mini-wave.

No. No, she didn't. No. That did not just happen.

I quickly look away, ignoring the very sudden flush of guilty sweat pouring from my body, pretending I am searching for something, anything, any*one* who is not her.

Which causes me to land on my brother, Jean, and his

idiot best friend, Aaron, seated in the deep back corner. They must have waited until everything began before slinking in. Oh joy.

At this point I decide I will definitely be better off focusing on the action below, as Marcus makes his point. "There is to be no chest-thumping tough talk, no name calling, and no cheap digs," Marcus' delivery slows, making eye contact with everyone, "but no sticky-sweet platitudes either. Knowledge, competition, and empathy are our goals."

Vikram steps back up. "A huge part of competing here is respect, integrity and . . ." Vikram's voice breaks off and he struggles to regain his thought. He takes a deep breath and exhales the rest of the sentence, "honor."

And as Vik continues talking, I'm no longer really listening because I'm searching my vocabulary for a word to describe him. It's a word I know I know, but can't grasp. Sad isn't quite right. But it's not morose, either.

I mine my mind, scrunching through the layers in my brain. And . . . got it. It is exsanguine. The word I want is exsanguine, without blood.

I was right. The game thief murdered him, leaving Vik-the-Cadaver in his place.

I side-eye Ari and see her leaning in, as though trying to physically will him through. On my other side, Imani's left fist is balled up, while her right hand is clutching Jimmy's sleeve. Is she clinging to him for support or to keep him in his seat? I can't tell.

As for me, my nails are digging so hard into my palms, there will be marks left. *Come on, Vik; you can do this.*

"Tonight after the challenge drops," Vikram drones on, "those of us on the engineering team will break into two groups. I will lead one group; Marcus will lead the other. We will open the challenge bag, do an inventory and, using the materials provided, begin to sketch our best design to accomplish the task."

Mercifully Marcus claps Vikram on his shoulder, relieving him of his portion of this presentation.

"So," Marcus claps his hands, working to boost the energy, lighten the vibe. "Once we have our mission, those of you not in either engineering or software, such as marketing and spirit peeps, will not be needed tonight. We will, however, need you tomorrow for about half an hour at lunch to begin work on our organizational info."

With that, we settle in to await the launch video via uplink. Cell phones are out, and everyone's calling someone, texting someone, or Snapchatting something. But not me.

I see Ari and Marcus trying to bolster Vikram and I feel an enormous, surging rush of anger. And in that rush is a tingling thought, swimming upstream from somewhere deep in the recesses of my mind.

And the more I stare down at Vik, the closer the tingle gets. *Better. Vikram deserves so much better.*

Faut pas toucher mes amis.

You do not mess with my friends.

I grab my phone and start to scroll. Respect. He deserves respect. Now I am seething. Like really furiously mad. This should have been Vikram's night. How dare someone hack into a game and rip off my friend, steal from him. It's so wrong.

I find it. *Contagion.* I hit download.

Here we go. "Noisypeacock3254?" Really? That's my default? Not happening. I scan the list of several active players' names, thinking, *who would I never, as in not ever, pretend to be?*

And when my eyes hit "viXXXen362436," I have my answer. Wow. A triple *X* to the Vixen. And to think somebody chose that. That is honestly scary. But it is also absolutely, definitively, not me. Not that "noisypeacock" is me either, but if I'm picking who I will never be, it should be my choice. Not for the inner-game-circuitry wizards to randomly select for me. Nope. Not happening.

It's like parents who give their kid a super geeky name and then shock (!), kid turns out to be a geek. Why are they surprised? It's predestination. Or maybe that's prede-termination. I'm not sure.

I am sure I am going to be vixen2729. With one *x*. Small letters. Don't want to be overly ambitious. This should be quite incognito enough for me.

From there, the tingle hits the wall, explodes, swirling my emotions until they become a metaphorical avenging mask and cape.

Faut pas toucher mes amis.

Which I will now use to cloak myself in the skin of vixen2729 and infiltrate this game, whereupon I will find and recover Vikram Patel's purloined loot.

I will be the epidemic this thief didn't see coming. I will be the, something . . .

. . . but I will have to be it later.

While I was downloading, the room shifted into high buzz. The monitor goes live. A countdown begins. As each second ticks by, any apprehensions we have about getting roped into this disappear. We all lean forward, three, two and . . .

. . . kickoff begins.

SIX

If I thought I needed proof from whatever powers that be that gamer-girl is my new destiny, this might just be it. But let me not get ahead of myself.

Because first, lights are dimmed, and from a few rows behind me, a raucous stomp cheer starts up and seats are now rocking. Stomp clap, stomp stomp clap, stomp stomp clap clap, stomp stomp clap.

Miraculously, row by row by row, we are all, kinda, sorta, more or less, on beat. And I know you are waiting for me to shrug and say something self-deprecating like, "well, except for my two left feet," but for the record, let me just state that while I may be a cardholding member of the Velma Valedictorians, I am the one with two dancing feet—you might remember my cherished LARPing spectators—and natural rhythm. Stomp stomp clap clap!

Stomp stomp clap.

Perfectly timed to the countdown ending! The main event begins. The challenge is ready to be issued, the gauntlet thrown. The room falls immediately, completely quiet as here we go . . .

Live action on the screen: We see a lone girl descending the stairs into a brick-walled basement. She finds a plastic-covered video arcade game, removes the cover, fishes in her pocket for a coin, feeds it into the machine, and is launched inside the game . . . where she finds an eight-bit throwback world waiting.

You know, the old-school, super-colorful, pixelated, console look. Totally Nintendo retro.

Here, the now-avatared young girl meets fellow avatar, Big Wig Bossi, who tells her she must find and collect seven power cubes in the *FIRST* realm. Then she'll be ready to play.

And she's off. Starting with a quick stop at the Critical Commodities Closet, followed by the Mentor Pool, finally netting directions to the Lotus Flower.

Here she comes upon a yoga-chillin', sukhasana-sitting Dr. Woodie Flowers, who magically pops out of the game and out of avatar shape, and into live form to chat about metacognition, which would be thinking about thinking, and stopping our sneaky brain.

Which of course, sets my sneaky brain right off.

I force myself to not start swiveling about, checking in case anyone, for any reason, is suddenly thinking of having their sneaky brain looking at me. Easier said than done.

". . . a team member who successfully sells a bad idea is not helping . . ."

Now there's some truth for you.

". . . as you build your robot you can learn an important lesson about truth's superiority over group think . . . pay attention to this." With that last word of caution, Dr. Woodie launches himself back inside the game, avatar girl sets back off, and cubes four through six are quickly gathered.

Which gets us to the seventh and final cube. A cube which will come straight from the rock star himself, an eight-bit, animated, Segway-riding Dean Kamen.

Yes, my friends, Mr. God of Robotics, inventor of Segways and other genius products, is speaking directly to us. Or at least his avatar is. And it's pretty intense. You can actually feel the awesomeness quotient radiating, nearly vibrating, throughout the auditorium.

I suddenly, fully grasp this isn't just some random school project, but that all across the United States and in over a

41

hundred countries around the world, we are all watching this same video . . . and we're all getting ready to compete.

I mean, I knew on some surface level it was an "international competition," but this is the first time I really, internally, get this enormity. I am awed by how freaking cool, and therefore kind of scary, this whole thing is.

Avatar Dean also exits the animated world for the live one, and as he does, his conversation becomes more personal, both about him, "My best ideas come when I'm enthusiastic and optimistic," and about us, "Use your time wisely. Be willing to take risks. Learn from your failures and keep moving."

And then Dean Kamen is wrapping up, and I'm leaning in, and what he says is something I intuitively know will be important to me forever. "Take the right risks."

That strikes home as I lean back and take my eyes off the screen for just a minute and realize everyone's caught in this same energetic glow. As though she can feel my eyes roaming, Imani turns to me, and we know exactly what we are both thinking without saying it out loud, *this really is freaking amazing.*

And now, the chit and the chat and the shtick are over.

This year's game is revealed.

An animated scoreboard screen appears, like the kind hanging from the ceiling at Madison Square Garden, bearing the name of this year's competition, in three separate lines, *FIRST* Power Up.

And cue the challenge!

A Day-Glo colorful animated graphic begins our journey through the competition. We watch as two alliances of video game characters/robots and their human operators, one blue, one red, find themselves trapped in an arcade game. To escape, alliances use power cubes to control switches and scales; pass power cubes through the exchange to earn power-ups, which are worth extra points, time and climbs; and finally ascend to face the boss.

At the start of each match, the plates of the scale and the switches will be randomized, so the course will not play the same way each time through.

The video continues, giving us a play-by-play from station to station, until finally we have traveled the course and get to the summation: the alliance that gains the most ranking points wins the match and defeats the boss.

And now we are on a live feed, on the actual playing field, which is called the arcade. As each component lights up, it is nearly as colorful as its animated counterpart.

It is here, among the engineers and the designers, that Dr. Flowers "levels up" and delivers to us all, the moment we came to get: The Code.

pLaY&4%R3aL!

Vik and Marcus scramble to enter it and boom, the game manual is released, and we are on the move.

Designers. Coders. Interested Parties descend en masse into Smitty's lab, all set to begin.

As soon as the huddling begins, I realize I've been had, but it's too late. Yes, as promised, the Twincesses and Hand Jive are two lab tables over, huddling on their stools, waiting for Marcus, but that separation will end as soon as we are finished designing competing bots and one is picked to be built.

Resigned to my fate, I look up and espy Jean and Aaron, who are still here, but haven't actually made it inside the room. They're kind of doing that door-hugging thing. It's like an epic cliffhanger. Will they be kicked to the curb, or will someone rescue them and let them join their table?

Which engenders another big sigh from me as I sort through my three immediate colliding thoughts: 1) my parents will kill me if I leave him out there; 2) he's actually pretty smart and way more into gaming than me, which might help; and 3) he is, alas, my brother. So if I kick him to the curb, that's fair play. But if someone else were to do it, I'd have to defend him.

Frankly this would be an easier decision if Aaron didn't remind me of a slurping Igor, which I am not allowed to say because Jean gets all defensive. Whatever.

I get it over with and wave them over, just in time for Marcus and Vikram to join us. Vikram is carrying reams of paper, while Marcus is balancing several large duffel bags.

"Okay, people, listen up," Marcus calls, focusing everyone's attention. "I have here the Kickoff Kit and the three drivetrains. Two of the drivetrains come from previous years, so remember they aren't all going to be exactly the same. Vikram has copies of the game manual, and an e-file will also be sent to you as soon as we get everyone's involvement coordinated."

"Memorize it." Vikram says. His delivery, I am relieved to report, is no longer depressive. A little terse, perhaps. The energy from watching the launch video and running to make copies seems to have revived his spirit, albeit not particularly playfully.

"There is nothing beyond these pages." Maybe a bit abrupt. "If you use even one 'disallowed' wire, screw, or anything else, we will all be disqualified."

And letdown! I was hoping he was going to finish by saying, "screwed." Then I could credit him with an epigrammatic flourish. Alas. Too late.

Time to design a bot.

SEVEN

Short-circuited. I am definitely feeling short-circuited.

Because my *après* school time now has this new team-coding commitment, I am, instead of sleeping, sitting on the floor, leaning back against my bed, feet pressed up against the wall, laptop propped open, busy trying to execute my Vikram rescue plan by leveling up the ladder of *Contagion*. Yes, this could be kind of a release from the cacophony of people invading my perimeter—Jean, Mae Ann, Scott, even Vik in his role as co-boss, but it's really not.

Not to mention, along with neglecting to calculate the loss of my afternoons, in my pique of caped crusader-ing, I'd also actually forgotten just how much I really don't like this game. Despise is a most apt descriptor, but I'm good with abhor as well.

So while my overtired self is busy underachieving on the leveling-up portion of this game, I am also struggling to keep up with the exciting *Contagion* global chat channel as it scrolls by.

whizacker3: nah dude. questing the whole way.

quadstra: tag them up.

Péter un plomb.

French for I am going crazy. Well, kind of. Not literally. Literally, it's French for I am breaking a fuse.

Which would be more accurate if I was freaking out going crazy rather than just sitting here bored off my gourd going crazy, but what can I say?

I do know this would be easier, and way more engaging if I happened to like *Contagion*, and if I had access to a second screen, aka my phone, which still, despite the lifting of our post-LARPing solitary confinement, remains plugged in the living-room outlet right outside my parents' bedroom wall.

And yes, I can answer that one for you, it is abso-freaking-lutely ridiculous that I can have my computer back, but not my phone. I believe the message is intended to be some not-so-subtle motherly reminder that *"Il y aura des consequences."* There will be consequences.

And, of course, they will hear it if it rings . . . or pings. Lip curl.

StarShine32: Nipah. Shit.

Snarl interruptus. I watch the shimmering net of the virus surround StarShine32, and as the disorientation begins and she, at least I think she, but I guess StarShine could be a he, or a they, whatever, spins, right into some stream of goo, and ew, there goes a foot. Ooh. Ow. Too close to the edge, Starshine . . . ignore the rules, suffer the consequences.

I give an internal laugh as I watch the expletives fly across the chat screen. You go right ahead and scream. I know just how you feel.

But I am nothing if not determined.

Ergo (another great underused word), welcome to night nine of my personal and still unsolved quest, The Case of the Purloined Plunder, wherein intrepid sleuth, that would be me, hunts for the person or persons who have made off with Vikram's stuff.

And yes, you probably thought this madness would pass. That it would all go away if not by the next morning, perhaps the following day.

Hey, I know I did.

I honestly thought by now I would be sitting here, catching up with, hmmmm, a bit of fanfic (you didn't really think I was going to say homework, did you?) or maybe, I don't know, bingeing *Scooby Doo* reruns, because you know, I ridiculously believed that maybe the game-maker would have sorted all this out and Vikram's inventory would have been returned and I would no longer be needed, but I would have huge brownie points for having had my friend's back. Perhaps might even have been the teensiest bit lauded. "No. Really." I hold my hands out and head bob just a bit, "It was no biggie."

Yes, I can admit to that.

I even thought I would help my heroism with a bit of action. Launched Twitter, followed @spitpolishgames, even thought to check out their feed, see if anyone else is busy screaming about being ripped off, or buying/selling stuff. Dead end. And with no comrades-in-misery appearing, I DM about Vik's stolen stuff. Had a great chat with "Dan" who is appropriately, respectfully appalled, and knows nothing. But he will "look into it" and get back to me.

I wonder if that will be in my lifetime. Because now I'm sitting here on night nine and I still got nada. Of course, it could still happen. At some point. Maybe. If the universe tilts another degree, or two, or ten, in my favor.

And as much as I want to tell myself to let it go, I am a dog with a bone, especially when it comes to my friends. *Faut pas toucher mes amis.*

I like to think this is what makes me a flawsome—highly aware of my flaws and yet, still awesome—individual.

So I'd like to think.

But first I'd have to confess a few things.

One, for the record, I did skip one night completely because my feelings got really bashed in, but that's getting ahead of myself. Two, I haven't actually gamed for nine nights. I didn't start off gaming. I began my adventure by thinking. Strategizing. Mulling my options. There seemed to be two best ways to catch a thief in the act, or at least red-handed, with the goods.

Catching them in the act seemed to me like a needle-in-the-haystack activity, but catching them with the goods, maybe not so much. All I need to do is find the gray market for *Contagion* and see if I can spot Vikram's loot for sale. Now I know it's not quite as simple as all that. I understand if there's a thief selling a couple of aspirin, I'm never going to be able to peg that back to Vikram, but a person doesn't get to the highest levels of a game without acquiring some very exclusive and rare artifacts.

Meaning, if I can find the right bazaar, I've got me a thief.

And according to Imani, retail therapy cures just about everything. I'm game. And yes, that pun is intended.

So for four nights in a row, this is exactly what I do. I hit up every site I can find selling anything and everything *Contagion*, and now I have zip. Just empty cart after empty cart.

It would seem the *Contagion* gray market isn't exactly a hubbub of bustling enterprise. There's not a whole lot out there, and virtually everything I manage to find is ordinary, all falling under the category I labeled the "lazy-player-load." You know, the "if you don't want to spend three hours to earn an antidote, buy it here, buy it now."

So while there's a bunch of entry-level antidotes or a ton of ten-second safety masks, there is nothing I can find that would have belonged to a top-tier player. There's also nothing listed to indicate whether any item is new and might be a precursor of a load to come.

Which really doesn't make any sense.

Why rip him off if you're not selling it?

Time for a new plan.

Night five I embark upon what becomes two even more frustrating nights of electronically eavesdropping, scanning through pages and pages of global chat, certain there would be some idiot griefer giving himself away and, hey *voilà!*

But no, no such luck.

Which brings me to night six. By the time I hit night six, all I hear is the Laugh of The Flynn, busy snickering at my self-imposed, rapidly failing enterprise. "Plan? You call this a plan?"

And although this moment is being brought to you by my own imagination, it is still enough to make me double down on my efforts, albeit with a bit of petulance, as I can't even have the satisfaction of slugging the imaginary Flynn in his imaginary shoulder.

It is now somewhere around three o'clock in the morning, when a desperate, trying-to convince-me-to-go-to-sleep brain cell gives one last pre-burnout power surge, and suddenly I know the first part of the answer.

Or maybe it's the first part of the question.

Although I'm already way past peak performance and happily hypnagogic, it's kind of fascinating how much genius can be delivered into this last gasp before sleep state. It's like your sleeping brain becomes a blank universe and then blindingly bright stars burst in. Even supernovas.

Which is why rather than think it out, I let the laptop slide down and continue upon my path to dreamland, where I am sure genius is waiting for me. Still on the floor, I am sliding down, pulling my blanket right off the bed and onto me, and flicker. My last memory is *I have it. I know I do.*

And rise and shine! Drumroll please. Welcome to what I like to call our school east locale, aka the right side of the building as you come through the courtyard. I texted everyone and we are now huddling, shivering, outside the school. Because while it isn't a freezing cold morning, it isn't all that warm either, a situation caused mostly by an imperative that school must continue to start at an ungodly hour, even if that means in the dark.

However, this morning I didn't care all that much;

49

everyone could shiver for just a minute. "Okay. I've got this."
I pause for dramatic effect, although not as long as I would
like. The wind that suddenly swirls through and around the
building blows (yes, pun intended) the moment.

"It's a Zero Sum Game."

Um, hello? Perhaps a small admiring head bob? Maybe a
knowing nod? Wow. Nothing. Other than four self-hugging,
feet-stamping, shivering bodies. Apparently they will need
more.

"So I get it. I know it's not that big a deal, more like a
curiosity."

And as I pause, a small memory comes back to me, that
late-night slight twist on the discovery. "You know, maybe
it's even the question, and not the answer. Which of and by
itself could be a clue." And I look from one to the next,
seeking signs of intelligent life. Wow. Knock knock.
Anyone home?

Finally, I turn directly to Vikram. "Look, I've tracked a
zillion sites and I can't find any of your loot for sale."

I continue to lay out my case, moving slowly person to
person. "Then I added two nights of doing nothing other
than perusing tons of global chat and again found zip. No
one else talking about being ripped off, no one talking
about hearing about anyone being stolen from, no one
talking about buying anything from anywhere."

Now I'm circling, putting it all together. "So my point is,
there's no benefit. Whoever did this is playing a zero sum
game, which makes no sense. Which means if we can solve
that riddle, we have the thief."

Granted, maybe this was clearer to me at three in the
morning, but I'm still pretty darn pumped. And I'm kind of
thinking, welcome to my moment of awesome . . .

Until I turn my beaming self to Vikram, who looks at me
like I have three heads. "Sid, did I ask you to do this?"

Horrible sinking feeling, the one where everyone within
a radius of twelve miles will know I have been outed as

some kind of lame fraud, emblazoned with a scarlet *L*, the ultimate accessory for losers, grabs hold. And tightens. Rendering me speechless.

And no one is saying anything because they are as stunned as I am, which leaves an opening just small enough for Vikram to explode through. "What makes you think I want your help?" And there's nowhere for me to hide. "Don't you get it? It's over for me. I don't care anymore. My stuff. My stuff . . . is all gone."

His hands are flying about, but then they lower, and Vikram steps up, closer to me and pulls himself up as tall and as straight as he can. "When I played, and I won, I did it the real way. Now it's all about Loot Boxes and money. And it's all crass."

In my brain I keep pleading with myself, *please don't cry, Sid. Don't let them see you cry.* And my desperate attempts to escape this mortification, calling out to my internal reserves, are failing miserably.

It's a curb-stomp battle my sucker-punched solar plexus never saw coming.

So I don't care when he spins around to leave. I am busy trying to get my breathing to hold steady. And I don't pay any attention as Ari is trying to reach out to him. So when Vikram turns back one last time, "And you, you're standing here, telling me there wasn't even a reason, that I was just a victim for nothing. Like that's some kind of freaking accomplishment."

I am not ready. My shields are still down.

But he's not done. Like a fighter pilot with one payload left, sensing an opening, he pulls up, thrusts, and delivers. "You know Sid, if you really want to help me, just show up and code. I don't need you to fix this. So just," Vikram pauses for a slight second, "just be who I need you to be. Okay?"

And with that last blow, he spins and leaves.

Before I can do anything—scream, cry, run, hide—I feel

the familiar arms of The Flynn spin me around, and I lean into his big, enveloping hug, burying my nose in his chest. "Sid, you know Vik doesn't mean a word of that. He's just so mad and you walked into it. It's like when you throw an interception and your parents say things like, 'You'll get 'em next time.' Or you strike out and they say, 'Good cut, son.' Even though they mean well, it sometimes feels even worse."

"So." I stay enveloped, taking a minute and letting Jimmy's warmth comfort me. Inhaling his familiar smell. "What do I do now?"

"You go find the asshat who stole Vikram's stuff." Jimmy hugged me tight and whispered to me, "Just like you're supposed to. Just like who you are."

EIGHT

Which is why I am still here, determinedly hunting for that needle in the proverbial haystack.

Previously on *The Hunt for Vikram Patel's Inventory*, we watched as suddenly sleuth-less Sid Rubin spent six nights achieving virtually nothing. Six nights and still no answers. Leaving us with one big question: Will Sid rise to the challenge and save her reputation, or will she be forced to turn her Velma card in?

Before I answered, I called for a time-out from our sponsor, me. I literally went undercover, having my hurt-feelings-take-the-night-off night, and burrowing deep.

Which was, I think, very merited.

So when you tally up my assorted highs and lows, I didn't actually start playing until night eight, which I have to admit did erase some of my ennui, making my quest feel more grounded.

And while acknowledging my woeful week, it's not like I haven't gained any "knowledge."

I have learned at least half the reason I hate this game is I don't like the art. For me, it has zero design appeal. The artists seemed to be undecided if this is their riff on a zombie theme or something else really dark. But it's without direction or elegance. There are lots of gray and purpled blacks and lots of chartreuse variations, which I suppose are meant to be sickly. But then the menus and pickups are done in hot pink, neon turquoise and even slime lime green, aka ye olde "fake-y happy colors."

It's all a bit clash-y.

As opposed to, you ask? I don't know, maybe some *steam-punk*!

Where everything is burnished and polished and smooth and elemental. Not intended for puking guts and oozing gobs of puss slurping their way across the screen, leaving their entrails behind.

I realize this may sound like I'm simply whining, but I'm really not. It's incredibly hard to play something for hours that doesn't stimulate your senses in a good way.

Taking a break, in between frantic texts from Imani and Ari, I slithered under my bed, dug out my prized stash of *Lumberjanes* for comfort, wrapped myself in my blanket, and sat and reread, and reread again, their commitment to "Friendship to the Max." A rallying cry to my inner troops, reminding us of why we have to be here, sitting in my room, committing to bad art and deadly outbreaks, despite being, ever so slightly, just a wee bit of a toxiphobe. Because this is what you do for friends(hip) . . . to the max.

Which makes me smile. And look up from the game to a picture of me with Imani, sitting on a shelf above my desk. Maybe Imani was right all along and I had been suffering from the PAPEs. And maybe I'm not so much hating on this game, but rather I'm having a relapse.

Nope. I shake my head. It's not a relapse. It's just your average sudden onset ague from Vik's tongue-lashing while being publicly intimidated.

OK. Sitting forward. Twisting to the left. Twisting to the right. I am definitely in need of some kind of adrenaline boost. But, since it is one fifteen in the morning, on a school night, heading to the kitchen for a cup of espresso would be a really bad move.

Then again, maybe I don't need coffee. Maybe I just need a life. You know, one that comes with a new girlfriend. A really cute, smart, funny, maybe even attainable, girlfriend who keeps me way too occupied for this.

And . . . right before I can digress right into that happy spot . . .

A giant slurping sound snaps me out of my reverie, just in time to see myself being eaten piece by piece by the Lassa Virus. *Gurgle. Slurp. Gurgle.*

Really?

Aw yuck. It actually just vomited me out! In one great green glob of goo. Now, that my friends, *that* is so freaking fourteen-year-old-boy gross.

But, take a deep breath. Inhale. Exhale. Because gross or not, it is a perfect example of why I will not be staying alive if I can't keep my mind in this game.

Anyone who games can tell you the first few nights of nearly any game you play are kind of easy and entertaining enough. So if you daydream, no biggie. The goal is simple. Suck you in, let you win, and then it begins to suck you dry. Feel free to insert an evil laugh here.

So leveling up from level one to five is fairly quick. Want to defeat the bubonic? Kill the rat. And fortunately, when you signed up and got your first pack, it had a piece of cheese and a trap.

I know, right? Low-lying fruit. Should be easy.

But the low-hangers are only the beginning; the out-breaks start to get more dangerous, trickier, and more time consuming. They become more resistant and more prone to change. There are fake cures, which only "appear to work" before they turn deadly. And charlatans abound, ready to sell you all sorts of potions and elixirs, which they "guarantee" will assist you with your recovery.

And all the while the viruses and diseases continue to cross-contaminate, linking up to increase both their epidemic power and their resistance, and eventually morphing themselves into something new and even deadlier. God I hate this game.

Which, as I said, is why I am still stuck being a level seventeen and now watching myself be regurgitated.

However, in my defense, it's not really about not liking the game, or even my lack of skill. It's because it's still less about playing than it is about maintaining constant contact with the chatter, listening in as gamers rant, rave, brag, boast, trade secrets or bs, and therefore expose themselves unwittingly to covert players. There's potential to suss out all manner of hidden action and clues.

But just like real life versus movie life, going undercover in-game is more yawnfest than derring-do, metaphoric cape or not.

I can't just drop it and steam ahead on playing, because I honestly have a weird sense that if there's going to be a tidbit to be had, as much as I hate scrolling it, the global chat channel is where I am going to find it.

And so for the eight-hundredth time, I rehash my logic in an effort to focus.

Somebody swiped Vikram's booty.

In theory, this could mean it's personal, but that makes really no sense in this game. I mean if Vikram had that kind of mortal enemy, who also had this kind of skill, even Vikram might have had some kind of clue. Which he obviously did not, even after several days of reflection.

Therefore I'm crossing off any sort of revenge motive, as that would be much more likely to be some weirder, not to mention really lame, movie plot than Vikram's universe could possibly warrant.

I even ran a check, as best as I could, on the players who gained positions while Vikram dropped down the rankings and then rose back up. None of those peeps seemed to chart out of nowhere, or leap several players in a single bound, or something that would make them suspect.

This leaves me with limited practical options, such as Vikram accidentally hitting a magic delete button, hidden by some sadistic game designer who said to himself, "one day some yutz will hit auto delete. This will be so much fun."

Yeah, not buying that one. Although in the it's-way-past-midnight overtired way, part of me thinks that would be kind of hysterical.

I'm also not buying some strange computer glitch. There's absolutely no traffic on anything remotely extrapolatable for that anywhere so, again, cross it off.

Which takes me back to my original thinking. It's a "for profit" enterprise.

Someone has to be farming the game. As in playing, collecting, and ultimately selling the stolen stuff. Now this theory is not one I like, because I can't find any signs of profiting—no listings or sell-offs.

I have set alerts everywhere and so far, nothing. I also can't find any other signs of profiteering popping up within the game. There've been no ransom demands, no gleeful "gotchas," no hidden hoaxes.

So again, the idea that it's a zero sum game is the only one that makes sense, but still leaves the why. And unless it was just for shiggles, then whoever hacked the game should still be playing. All I need now is for the reason to unveil itself . . . somehow.

I have just two words for myself, circle jerk. Or not.

Jax21: wtf! Grinding in ruff by the caves and a freakin' giant thing just swooped in, killed the x-or36 contamination in one swing.

Hello! Come to Sid, you lovely global chat thread.

There are certain contagions that are outrageously difficult to beat, and a solo player would need to be leveled up near the top to have something in their arsenal that might be of use. And if they do, and they can defeat these outbreaks, there are all sorts of bonus bumps and bounty available, some of which is in the riches-beyond-compare category for gamers.

So I wait and I watch the stream continue with its usual

assortment of boring, stupid jock-ularity lurking until Jax21 finally resurfaces.

Jax21: I'm telling you dude, couldn't tell hypo/sword.

Bam! And now I'm all over it.

vixen2729: was it blue?

Jax21: confirmed.

Wowzerhole. Fluck me.

Jax21: you know it?

I ignore him. I've got what I need.

I remember when Vikram won this blue thing. It was maybe one, even two years ago now. I remember it being back when I thought he was a sycophantic ass, certain his head bob was created by his slinky-for-a-spine. Definitely going back to the days before Ari, thankfully, got him a calcium infusion.

I know it was a Monday morning. Vikram came into homeroom all jacked up about winning this thing.

"It's called a SwHypo because it has both antitoxin and weapon capabilities." Vikram circled the room, showing off his newly acquired treasure. "It's the only one in the game." Blah. "It was a lottery win." And blah. "I played for thirty-six straight hours, almost all weekend." And blah.

This litany went on for days; I kid you not. I can't even say who I wanted to kill more, him or me.

And thus it is perfectly, bitterly, ironic that this stupid SwHypo would be the answer . . . or the clue. I'm not sure yet.

I am, however, absolutely sure it means either the thief, or the buyer, is active and playing. I can't imagine it would be a buyer at this point. For starters, if you were the buyer, I think I might have found some evidence of you before this.

And more importantly, there's still too much game left to farm and if you had the SwHypo, you'd be one pretty freaking invincible farmer.

NINE

Who needs sleep? I mean really, way overrated. I bolt straight out of bed at seven this morning, having first gone to sleep somewhere after two. And it's a Saturday! And it feels great!

I'd found a whopping clue *and* I leveled up to eighteen, which happens to be the Jewish numerical assigned as "life," which I think we might deem a rather timely portent.

Flush with success, I call for a meeting, sending out our urgent, no-time-to-explain-meet-me-here text, which is an emoji of a "thing" followed by a number.

It's our newest system, one not found in Emojipedia, because we designed it right after our last system was imploded by our parents. There are several emojis to choose from, each designating a specific location, none of them featuring an eggplant or a peach. In this case, I used a plate plus 1. One o'clock, Platitude. It's efficient if not deep.

I'm not particularly happy about having to wait until one, because we all know I am so all over this, but it can't be earlier. I mean I suppose it could, but then there would be no Jimmy because he has a game tomorrow, which means he has morning practice today. And I am not doing this without him. Not going to happen.

Vikram and I have been more or less fine working together on the robotics challenge, but it's a little on the polite side of fine.

If I'm fully confessional here, even in my excitement,

calling the meeting has me a little bit jittery. Last time, I distinctly remember, it didn't go so well—especially for me.

But it's done. So now all I have to do is kill some time without bouncing off enough walls that there would be questions.

Questions would be bad.

Can't have questions.

"Sidonie?"

Geez! It is so unpleasantly weird how I can even *think* about avoidance and she's right there. And not like, "oh she has eyes in the back of her head" there. No, it's way worse. It's more like she has eyes in the back of *mine*!

I take a calculated moment to un-grit my teeth. Work on relaxing the jaw so I can achieve vocal nonchalance. "*Oui*, Mama?"

Not bad. A little pitchy, but still in the "sounds like me" zone.

"Can you please open the door?"

Eye roll. Un-grit teeth. Again. Open door. Lean out. Gear up half smile. Raise eyebrows. There's Mom, down the hallway, having stepped out from the kitchen.

"You know I dislike yelling through a closed door." And dramatic pause, while we both make sure I heard that.

"I'm setting out breakfast. Are you planning to be here to join us, or are you heading out somewhere else?"

Breakfast? I hadn't given that much thought. And now that she's mentioning it, breakfast sounds great. It's not like I need to rush off. "Nope. I'm in."

And oddly enough it is lovely. Croissants from a little patisserie around the corner, fresh fruit, yogurt. Chitchat with the folks, who are so miraculously chill there is no grilling to be had. Note to self, pop in for breakfast more often. Turns out to be an incredibly indulgent and civilized way to start the day, which today is topped off by Jean having to leave first to go somewhere I don't really care, other than now his thinking we are somehow buddies and

60

trailing after me can be officially removed from my list of details to take care of. And for just a moment, it really is all so zen.

But you know, zen and I are such fleeting friends.

And just like that, zen jilts me. Gone. Goodbye. Leaving me pacing up, down, left, right, waiting for one o'clock, a consequence of having arrived half an hour early. I now know it takes eleven steps to walk from the front door of Platitudes to the street using an average stride. If you walk north-south in New York, it's about twenty blocks to go a mile. I'm thinking I have already logged at least a 5K.

I could probably be more precise but I am still working to convince my parents an Apple watch is not a luxury, but a necessity.

Yeah. So far it's not really working for me.

I did actually go inside to grab a booth in the back, but sitting by myself downing two cups of coffee unfortunately seemed to unleash the Vikram angry face, setting it loose and flitting wildly across my brain. With each sip, he grew larger and loomed angrier, setting off a bout of shrinkage-of-my-nerves, which I tried calming by alternating aimless incessant knee bouncing with crossing my leg under my body to stop said knee bouncing. Mercifully I finally had a lightbulb thought.

Waiting out front will be a better use of my completely over-caffeinated, overwrought energy.

Which is why I am out here pacing, up and down and boom, hit the corner, swing around the lamppost, turn, and boom, seven zillion steps later, approaching me from the other side, is Ari.

About five feet before reaching me, she stops and pulls up, so I stop and pull up. Suddenly I am under her micro-scope, being looked at from top to bottom, and then bottom to top. Full eyeball examination.

And then, before I can say anything, Ari lunges and shrieks, wrapping me up in her arms—and into her rather substantial—uhmmm, chest, and gives me a big, wild, side-to-side rocking hug. "I knew you'd do it."

"Do what?" I do manage to ask despite feeling a bit at sea—and no, not from the rocking motion. It's hard to maintain any kind of linear thought, other than trying to think not to sink, straight down and into . . . Nope. No sinking.

Sometimes I don't think Ari remembers the power of her "girls." Those Double D's. On me. Not in general. In general I know Ari knows fully well the power of those girls. I've seen them in action. No. No. No. Not personally. Get your mind out of the gutter here. I was referring to her LARPing attire. Wowzerhole.

Then again, really, who am I kidding? Ari probably knows exactly what those girls do to me. Getting weak from lack of air. Self, there will be no passing out.

"I knew you'd find a way to get Vik's toys back."

I am about to protest that I really didn't actually do all that much, that I don't have his winnings back, at least not yet, when Ari grabs me up again.

This time I try and keep the crushing, rocking, overstimulating motion at bay by focusing my one unmushed eye on the horizon, which is not easy when your glasses are part of the Tilt-a-Whirl.

But eye-smush and all, as I am mercifully being released, I spot Imani and Jimmy making their way down the block. Fortunately they are too far down the street to see me straighten my glasses, realign my shirt, and buckle my knees. I attempt to politely snort up my loosened nasal membranes and regain some sense of, uh, sangfroid just as Vikram also arrives.

As we all meet in the middle, Vikram walks solemnly up until he is directly in front of me. "I'm sorry, Sid. I was an ass."

I'm proud of myself. I don't flinch. I just look directly at him. "You hurt me."

"I know." Vikram stands there and waits. No more words. No excuses. No explanation. Just the acknowledgment.

Which is all I need. "Okay."

And with that we are all smiling wide, and within minutes, we are once again the fearsome five, crammed around the big table in the back of Platitude, gawking over a computer with coffee and black and whites for all. No robo-peeps. No group hug, let's go team, rah-rah kind of thing. Nope. We are hashtag Throwback Thursday-on-a-Saturday.

And I am so loving today.

Enough so that I just ordered an honest to gosh black and white malted to go with it. Color me nostalgic. Chichi, foo-foo coffee shop hangouts don't have them, you know.

And I'd like to tell you that my week of playing was worth the expression on Vikram's face, but I have to say it wasn't.

Not to say he wasn't stunned, and just to confirm, he absolutely wasn't angry, and not to say everyone else wasn't perfectly impressed, but really, when you play for days on end and wind up more or less finally passing out hearing a *slurp, chomp* followed by, "Bile . . . Bile . . . Fed for a While . . . Ha Ha Ha" ringing in your ears, incorporating itself into your less than fun dream, even one's own giddiness and Vik's happy face doesn't fully achieve the even-stevens.

I did manage to miraculously defeat the Lassa and level up to eighteen before I hit upon that charming chomp, slurp couplet. Which was key because, just between us, if it had taken me all those nights to hear those lines and I was still stuck on like, level five, we would so not be here this morning. I do have some pride. Because even though my discovery of the SwHypo is impressive, of and by itself, it's not enough.

Knowing someone has stolen your property and getting it back are two entirely different things. And getting it back needs a lot more backup. Or at the very least, more than just me.

I know I'm not the best gamer on the planet, although I would like to be clear I'm also not the worst. I can, however, live stress free knowing I won't be taken in the *NBA 2K* League draft. Because while I would like to think I could be SSSniperwolf or Cupquake, I believe the appropriate snark would be "in my dreams." I do take some consolation in believing I could outcode them all, even if I can't outscore them.

Hey, sometimes it's the little thoughts that count. Like, you know, are there any small oceans?

And your first thought is to snort and say, "nooo," but then you realize, well yes, there are, if only metaphorically. As in I woke drowning in the ocean of pus released into my body by the KroniK PP virus, which is what happens when at level fifteen you get caught in the tidal bore of pneumonia plus pulmonary disease, and you have no defenses for it!

Yes my friends, even here, while glowing in my achievement, I am still hating this game.

But now, now I have backup. Here we are, sitting with everyone's laptop on the table, having all created names and signed up to play. Well, everyone except Vikram. Vikram is on the outside of our lovely red pleather aka vinyl booth, leaning over everyone else's shoulders, working to jump-start each of the newbies so they will quickly get a few items to help them play.

By the time we hit the three-hour mark, it is two hours and thirty minutes past recognizing who games and who does not. Jimmy is already up to level twelve, and with a few Vikram pointers I have actually managed to come close to defeating the body mucus and nearly leveling up to nineteen. Which is not the same as actually leveling up, but better than not lasting five seconds before succumbing—repeatedly.

Under ordinary circumstances this would be sad enough to maybe even be pathetic, except I am playing with Imani and Ari, and they, well, let's just say it, they are never going to be much help.

Not that being useless gets anyone off the hook. Nope. Ari gets to hunker down in the rough near the cave, keeping an eye out for a reappearance of the SwHypo, while Imani culls through the Global Chat to see if there are, or were, any other messages about the big blue.

"Arghhhhhh!" My fit interrupts everyone's concentration as I slap at my keyboard and watch myself get taken out for the sixth time by the deadly Marburg virus. And I was *this* close!

The small side glances of sympathy do nothing for me.

I honestly think it might be a better use of my time, and really, all our time, if I were to join Ari and Imani. But who am I kidding? That's so not going to happen. I know, deep down, even if I suck, even if I hate this game, I want to be part of the action.

I crack my knuckles and shake out my fingers. To quote *The Grey*, "Once more into the fray."

Of course, I don't remember Liam Neeson weeping to himself as he said this.

TEN

We didn't find our thief that day, or for the next entire week. Which wasn't for lack of trying, just for lack of time. Between classes, after school, and even *before* school can be summed up in one word: robotics.

Since the night the challenge dropped, things have been moving at lightning speed. We do not have a lot of time and there is a ton of stuff to be done.

I am rather chuffed (so love that word; it's somehow "puffier" than just the old "I'm rather pleased," and yet still falls, just barely, but nonetheless under the level of overly obnoxious braggadociousness) that our table's design was deemed the better choice, and the assembling of the robot actually came together pretty seamlessly.

And in one of those shocking twists I would never have seen coming, Imani volunteered to be the Chief of Construction, responsible for building our entire practice run. In order to compete, we need to know our robot can perform all the required tasks and then we tweak for time, accuracy, etc. Since each year's task is completely different, new "sets" are always required and mostly need to be scavenged from previous years and anything else that can be scavenged up. Well, all the years of theater gave Imani more blueprint/painting/hammering/building-to-spec experience than most of the shop peeps, and, we got the added bonus of her having an experienced crew she could cajole into helping, along with "flats" galore for repurposing.

It also gave us two additional mentors, Pops aka Mr. Rabon, one of the school's part-time shop/part-time aide teachers and Ms. Bessette, the drama/art teacher.

Which is all great stuff.

Now, not because I was thinking train wreck around the curve or anything, but you know, I did sneak into her first team meeting, because, well, just because, which is how I not-so-accidentally stumbled upon what might secretly become my favorite part of this exercise. Imani's previously well-kept secret, known only to her besties, is now officially out of the box and known by all. And no, not her math woes. Everyone already knows about those. What everyone doesn't know is that underneath all that charm Imani hides an incredibly, and occasionally savage, bossy streak.

There is a reason she is the prima donna.

"Listen up, people." Imani is strutting back and forth in front of her crew, having gathered them in a section of the grandstands that line the gym. "There are six weeks until the curtain goes up and we debut our competition robot. That means we need to be in full dress rehearsals, every set ready and operable, in less than four weeks. If you are not in a class and you are not sleeping, you are building. Understood?"

I know she thinks actress, but she is destined to become a director. Not incompatible.

"First up, I want black tape down on the floor marking the arcade field. Make sure it is exact. After that we will get to marking off the scale, the alliance wall, the fence, etc., each in their own color." Imani pauses and reaches down into a canvas tote bag. "See this book?" She holds up a black loose-leaf binder. "When you finish taping a section, write down the color tape and the exact measurement you used. And then," pause, "you initial it."

I can see the "what did I get myself into" reactions growing, so before I actually burst out laughing, I'm thinking—one, I need to get out of here now, before she spots me and there is hell to pay, two, whatever you do, people, do yourselves a favor and do not let her have the walkie-talkies or even worse, the megaphone, and three, you know, Imani-in-charge really rocks those coveralls, construction boots, and tool belt. Totally sexy on her.

Um, hello! I am her lesbian best friend. It is my absolute duty to notice.

And with that happy-making thought, slipping away, I spot The Flynn backing out a different door and heading down the hallway.

He turns, sees me. I shrug. He nods. Then he tilts his head toward the door he's just backed out of and I nod, acknowledging my own complicity, allowing him the eye roll of "wow." I screw my face up with that "oh yeah, I know, not pretty" look and nod.

And as we body-language chat, Jimmy walks his way over to me with, suddenly, something. Maybe intent. Maybe he's walking with intent. Or maybe just seriousness. You know, Flynn with no trademark smirk seems wrong. I resist my sudden urge to take a step back while running my hand through my hair.

"Hey Sid?"

"Yeah?"

Jimmy fidgets about, and I realize, whatever it is, he's nervous. Which of course, to me, means I should be nervous. So by now, I really just want to scream, "spit it out," but I don't. I wait.

And now, pushing himself from the wall back to in front of me, with one big exhale, Jimmy finally begins. "Look, I'm not sure the best way to say this, so I'm just gonna put it out there. I miss you. I mean football season was always crazy, but now I also have a girlfriend. And don't get me wrong, I like having a girlfriend, it's great. I mean, she's great." Unconscious brief pause for a smile. "Look, I don't have to tell you that." Jimmy stops the rush of words, takes a deep breath, and gets to his point. "But I miss hanging with just you sometimes."

I look at Jimmy, who's once again standing tall. His half-grin is back, but unaccompanied by a smirk, and I feel what he's just said flow right through me. And I realize it's everything. It's even things I didn't know.

I feel the corners of my mouth turning up. "The glowing owls?"

This makes Jimmy's smile go full on. The glowing owls are in Herald Square, and when we were younger, it was such a big deal to see them. It meant we were out "after dark." He nods. "It's a date."

And with that we head off, each to officially report we have sneak previewed the beginning of what will soon be a fully operational mock course. Unofficially, and without a need to report, Flynn and I have also sneak previewed our future. Pursuing the balance that will keep us OB's, "Original Besties," as life keeps happening. It's a very grown-up moment.

But I digress. Rather happily.

During which time, Imani's triumphant return-to-the-stagehand, as she likes to call it, unexpectedly freed up Marcus, allowing him to focus and drill down on executing the business and marketing plans, a separation of tasks that seemed to make Jimmy very happy, Vikram, not so much.

Because, while I thought for sure Ari would wind up working on the spirit side of the endeavor, if not becoming the Spirit Leader, in the second twist of the twists I didn't see coming, she chose to work on the business committee, that same committee headed by Marcus.

I vaguely remember Ari looking at a slightly perturbed Vik and muttering something about "if I'm doing it for the college resume, I might as well make it count."

Didn't seem to particularly mollify Vikram. If you recall, I did mention Marcus's near-mythic ability to flirt.

So there were two twists. But as we all know, the old rule of three requires there to be one more twist I didn't see coming. And it is the biggest shocker of all.

The twincesses actually split up. And I mean *split up*. Mae Lee went and joined the spirit squad, which of and by itself has to be the most random thing ever, and, get ready for it, they, the twincesses, even came to school in non-matching outfits.

I know!

And they weren't even non-matching but still sort of close. No. They were pink miniskirt and white boots with heels versus slime-lime jeans and high tops. Whether by design or not, there was no way you could miss this momentous occasion even if you tried. And if by any chance I was too dense, or too oblivious, or too so-not-interested (!) to take note, Janelle apparently considered it a public service to make sure everyone, myself included, is up to speed on this extraordinary occurrence.

Which is fine. But what bothers me is what I don't know, and I am definitely not asking, which is "are we to file this under 'miracles still happen' or 'something wicked this way comes'?" Either way, I felt a need to check my horoscope, and run a quick search on all doomsday prophecies I could find. So far, nothing seems too imminent.

I'm sure if that changes, I will know soon enough.

Until then, we are sitting here, in the science lab, working as fast as we can to get our bots up and running at whatever their optimal level will be. Which means I am frantically writing and rewriting code with the two people who you might remember give me a case of the yips, Scott and Mae Ann.

If I was Shakespeare and I had a petard, it would so be hoisted.

But surprisingly, in some ways this is better, and not surprisingly in some ways worse, than I imagined.

When we are in the midst of coding, it's all pretty good and generally, even funny, in a geek-tech paradise kind of way. Like Scott saying, "use a foo," or when the three of us

70

began singing, "Ninety-nine little bugs in the code, ninety-nine little bugs . . . you fix one bug, compile again . . . one-hundred little bugs in the code."

And it's great. This camaraderie. This no holding back, nerds are we, skillfest.

Until I realize I am leaning over Scott's shoulder and Mae Ann is sitting just a tad too close and then, well, I heebie-jeebie all over again. Blech.

I am ashamed to admit, I sometimes worry if I let my guard down with them, my very fragile, borderline cred will take a hit. I know. I said I am ashamed. But sometimes high school is hard.

However, awkward alliance or not, we are in it to win it, and progress we are making. With Jimmy, Trey and a bunch of the guys at practice, and Marcus off with the business gang building a marketing plan and soliciting industry partners and sponsors, Vikram is who we currently enlist to drive our alpha bot. And when you're coding things like "move forward an inch," he's as perfectly capable as the next guy.

So our first key mission is trying to grab a power cube from the floor. This entire arcade is built around power cubes, and our efficiency with them will be key.

So first the manipulator must lower into position:

```
protected void execute(){
        Robot.cube.Manipulator.deploy.set(Value.kForward);
    }
```

We look up. And nothing.

Vik looks over at the three of us, we look at each other. Look at the code. And there, staring back at us, is the one dot too many. If it could scream out neener neener neener, it would. Scott makes the adjustment and:

```
protected void execute(){
```

```
Robot.cubeManipulator.deploy.set(Value.kForward);
}
```

You know, it occurs to me as I am sharing this with you, for my non-coding friends, this might sound painful. But it isn't. It's magical. I mean, think about it. We are taking a line of words and squiggles, and with them we control the ability of a machine to do exactly what we want it to.

There's a programmer's joke that says an algorithm is a word used by programmers when they do not want to explain what they did. I don't buy that. I just think what we do is hold the ability to fly in our fingertips. It's really pretty freaking awesome.

And it would be even faster and even more awesome, not to mention way more accurate, if I didn't keep making Scott sit like, two feet away from me at all times. And I kind of feel bad about that. It's not like he's done anything wrong, and he can really code, but some icks are harder to get over than others. And I am doing the best I can. Hey, a few years ago I literally would have made him wear gloves.

```
protected void execute(){
```

Okay, where were we? Right. Now we need to get the cube to move inside. Not quite as glamorous as flying, but so it goes . . . *abracadabra* . . . cube into manipulator . . .

```
Robot.gearManipulator.intake.set(1);
```

. . . Scott types it in. I signal a thumbs up to Vikram. And yes, high fives all around, we are starting to build some rhythm here.

ELEVEN

But not here.

In spite of my *Contagion* thief-at-large challenge, I have officially declared this Friday night to be a working-on-my-new-cosplay-outfit for the always exceptional, always competitive New York City Comic-Con night. Because, a cosplayer's got to do what a cosplayer's got to do. Before it's too late. And you're stuck with last year's outfit.

And thus my friends, virtually every single piece of clothing, whether used previously as a cosplay piece or not, is strewn across my bed, dresser, desk and floor, each forming one of twelve or thirteen piles of possibilities.

Given the eclectic accumulation of pieces I glommed from our last LARPing-go-round, now spread out directly before me, it occurs to me I might be able to spare-parts my way into the coolest Edward Scissorhands ever.

Or at least since the original.

And while there is that challenge of the best way to craft the hands, I am thinking I have a plan for that. It involves scissors, lots of scissors, and soldering . . . lots of soldering.

Which I don't actually know how to do.

Which is why it is still not a brilliant plan. Yet.

Well that, and also because I really am torn. Part of me wants to step it up, use what I can salvage, trade an extra pair of goggles I have somehow managed to accumulate for an eye patch and go as Franky from *Sky Captain and the World of Tomorrow*. I know, not a particularly great movie, but digitally so ahead of its time, and the production design and costume designs are truly standout. I mean, this would be pretty freaking awesome.

But as with most awesomeness, there are potential drawbacks. In this case, the number one drawback is presenting myself as Angelina Jolie. It's a wee bit, ahem, intimidating. Without knowing if Jimmy and Imani will come with me, it feels a bit thin. Now if they would come and be Polly and Sky Captain, it would so rock.

Some cosplay choices just work better as a group.

And yes, I can hear you. I do know I could just ask them, but every now and then I realize I am still adjusting.

Not that I don't think they wouldn't come or something, but it's different. You know, back in the day, when we went as just a bunch of friends, it was easy. We were a trio. Now, we're a two plus one. Which is a very different beast.

So I don't know. Yes, I could ask them, but I'm not sure if I want their answer. If I don't ask, then it's like I'm making a choice. But if I ask and they say no, it's a knife to my heart.

And ping. Thank you, whoever you are.

Plate + 7. TF Commands.

TF Commands. Why yes sir, Mr. Flynn, sir. What the "capital T, capital F" aka The Flynn commands, we minions serve to answer.

My thought was apparently rapidly seconded, and thirded, by the chorus of "thumbs up" pinging. And for a random split second I think, hey maybe I should go ghost, text and say something like I'm busy . . . but, even before I finish it, I think who am I kidding? Everyone is fully aware that I have a little Fear Of Missing Out aka FOMO issue, so I think everyone knows I won't be letting them have an emergency meeting without me.

And yet, before I can even ping back, another ping comes through. This time it's only for my eyes. All it says is, "Hey Sid . . . Never Leave Your Wingman."

He's quoting *Top Gun*. The Flynn is freaking quoting *Top Gun* at me. I don't bother to answer; he knows I'm in.

I look at the piles of clothes, strewn everywhere.

Oh well. Not much to do about that now.

I reach for my wallet.

Shit.

Back to the piles of clothes, diving in, pushing them to either side, not caring as at least half of them hit the floor, until I finally find bottom, unbury my coat and wallet, and race for the front door, yelling out, "Hey Mom, I'm off to meet the gang."

Before I can get the door slammed behind me, her voice calls back, "Curfew, Sid."

Yeah. Yeah. And slamming.

TWELVE

And now flying in the door.

Judging by the multiple baskets of fries, I am clearly not the first to arrive, which is personally disappointing and possible only because I had to stop and reload my metro card. A circumstance that was not only annoying, but time-consuming and ridiculously old-fashioned. I know somewhere there's already an app for that. And they, whoever they are, need to get on it.

But despite my delay, upon arrival I find I am not the only one who had their plans summarily interrupted by this alert. As I slide into the booth, Ari is texting she will get here as soon as she and Marcus are done with some investor meeting. Vikram—in a genuinely unguarded, and ridiculously unlikely, moment—actually snarls, which I have to say is kind of cute coming from him. And funny.

And then forgotten.

Because there will be no time for teasing, taunting, or torturing.

The suddenly sphinxlike royal Flynn awaits. He has tucked himself in the rear of the booth, giving him use of both the booth back and the wall, so even as he is reclining he is gaining posturing leverage, all while staring directly at me, his enigmatic half grin on full display, his hands clasped behind his head, just waiting for me to pick up what he is throwing down.

I look over at Imani, then back to Vikram, then back to

Jimmy. Full Force Focus. Satisfied, his hands unclasp as he leans forward and picks up his phone, which had been positioned face down on the table. Now, using his thumb and index fingers to hold the edges of his phone, he places his elbows on the table, and painfully slowly inches them forward, as though his screen is zooming toward me. Well, zooming via the world's most exaggerated, slowest-motion process ever. And then—

Then, I am Lost to the Wow.

Holy Moly, Batman. The Flynn did it. He found it. And even from this distance I know it is a ridiculously good find. Which, considering I have invested only about, I don't know, a gazillion hours of my life battling these stupid, asinine contagions, seems revoltingly unfair.

And Jimmy Flynn knows it. "Hey Sid," the phone inches closer, "read it and weep."

I reach; he snatches it away. *What are we, three?* At least Imani has the decency to roll her eyes and slap him on the shoulder.

Hey, I know it's not much, but I happen to like a display of solidarity—when it's with me.

But I get it, loud and clear. His royal smugness is in control. *Carpe diem*, Mr. Flynn. I give him the slightest of head bobs. Seize your day.

And with that, I get myself botoxicated, which involves plastering on my fake smile while I open my eyes so wide they force my forehead to tighten right into my scalp, and sit just a touch forward. Now ready, I give a sweep with my open-palmed hand.

The table is his.

"So Sid." Jimmy deliberately moves his face-down phone, this time just far enough to be out of my reach, and begins to tell, or shall we say exaggerate and embellish, his story. "There I was, cruising around at Level Forty-One, or was it Forty-Two? Hmmmm. Let me think for just a second."

Flynn is now pausing, taking time to make his thoughtful, scowly face while the fingers of his right hand begin to pop up, providing a fake count as a companion to his annoying chatter.

"Football practice. Math homework. English paper. No, I was right. Only Forty-One. And as I cruised, I was at plotting how I could best level up yet again before hitting the sack, when I espied what one might call unusual activity."

Oh yeah. He is going to milk this moment for everything he can. Can't actually say I blame him. I might as well self-medicate with some grease. My hand locates the nearest basket of fries.

"I pulled up and studied it for just a brief moment when I realized there was a game afoot."

Afoot? Really? He gets to use *afoot*? I am equal parts annoyed at him and annoyed at me. So I am totally annoyed. Which allows my botoxication to desert me, and my barely hidden snarkitude to penetrate rapidly through my hastily crafted mask.

Suddenly Jimmy leans in and is now talking like a really bad Sean Connery or something, "Ay lassie, afoot. Picture if you will, an attempt to conquer the beastly plague what guards the cave, but not for a single brave player. Nay. There were three of them, using each other to spin the plague before it could unleash. It was clever. But the plague was faster."

Now because we (that would be you and I) are now old, rather dear friends, I will summarize what took me nearly thirty minutes of blow-by-blow, incredibly badly accented event-telling, to absorb.

Jimmy managed to get himself into the cave by working as a wingman to another player. And because Vikram has been there and done that, we all knew this particular cave is one of the few places in this game where, when you defeat a certain viral combo outbreak, it lets you "sign" your accomplishment. And to the best of our knowledge, between our trying to monitor the global chat and such, the last player in, and thus owner of the "signature," had been the holder of the SwHypo.

So Jimmy crashes in on this guy's tail and grabs a screen-shot of said signature from the cave wall before the tailed-into-the-cave-dude overwrites it, putting his own name up. Which, as soon as he does, releases some new antidotes not generally available, so it's a pretty big moment, and not one where you, the interloper, can really say, "hey, mind not signing that while I get some additional pics for just a sec?"

Okay, now you are up to speed. And thankfully, Jimmy has finished embellishing every bell and whistle and can now reveal the cave signature picture on his phone to an appropriate round of *oohs* and *ahhs*.

So I'm not sure what anyone else was expecting, but I was hoping it was going to be something like Frank12 or MarySue3.

Nope. No such luck.

"Hey, handsome stranger . . ."

As Ari's hello registers, Vikram turns around for what will be at least two minutes before there is a break for air, which means the audience attention is now fractured and I motion to Jimmy to pass the phone directly to me.

And I see . . . well . . . a Chinese symbol. Like the kind you see on one of those game tile things. "Come on guys, it's a what-do-you-call-it?" I know this. They have those tournaments in Bryant Park. Think Sid. Think. Mah-jongg. That's it. "It's a mah-jongg tile."

A rather blurry mah-jongg tile, which means if you take your two fingers and enlarge it, you only make it worse.

I try squinting. Useless. I release my fingers, get up and let Ari into the booth, pass the phone to her and Vikram, never breaking eye contact with The Flynn.

Who in turn shrugs. "Hey, I don't know. It's a screen grab; focus should have been fine."

79

Fair enough. And the Chinese makes sense. I wondered why whoever this was has no letters in their user name. Only numbers and symbols. I assumed this was someone playing incognito. But if the thief is using a foreign language keyboard, like Chinese, it wouldn't have the English alphabet on it. And that fits much better.

Or, it could be whoever it is has a thing for random numbers.

Okay, back to the tile. I swivel right to our Princess of Languages, Imani, who is caught playing with her necklace in her mouth, zip-lining its charm back and forth.

"Oh no. Do not be looking at me." Imani's chain drops as her eyebrow raises. "I already said I haven't got a clue. For starters, I do not play mah-jongg and there are, I think, five Chinese languages, of which I speak maybe two dozen words of Mandarin. And speaking two dozen words is nowhere near the same thing as being able to read the symbols."

And while we're digesting that, even before I know I am thinking it, I say, to my utter disbelief, "What about the twincesses?"

Really. That actually just came out of my mouth. Ew.

If Ari saw the shiver of disgust, she kindly paid it no mind. "Won't help. At least I don't think it will. They don't really speak very much Chinese."

Now something about this strikes me as puzzling, starting with how does she know that, but before I can start grilling her, Imani interrupts. "Look, forward me the pic and I'll send it to Fenny."

Which we do. Which, in turn, releases me to return to what would have been my topic at hand, *Hey Ari, how do you know the twincesses don't read Chinese?* But yet again, before I can ask, we are interrupted, this time by our waitress who leans across the table, bringing a large cherry Coke to Ari.

Ari takes the paper off the straw, swirls the ice twice, takes a sip, looks up and demands, "I hate to interrupt this moment, but I need to know something. I need to know why it is men think that when they walk in a room and you are introduced and they say, wow, beauty *and* brains, there is somehow a compliment in that?"

The silence is deafening. Uncomfortable. Fidgety.

I know I got nothing, because she's right. But more than that, I don't think I ever stopped to think about how hard it must sometimes be to be Ari.

I think we are all slightly relieved when the *Facts of Life* theme song ping pierces the silence. The "you take the good, you take the bad" ring is suddenly like the best ring ever.

And Imani gives a little nervous laugh. "Hey, she was my boarding school mate," and checks her phone, upon which she gives a squeal. "Oh my god, Fenny's actually here. In the city. Can meet us at nine o'clock." And with that, she looks around, "Where?"

Which is how we, as in Imani and me, find ourselves huddling outside a building, + stack of books + 2, code text for the Stephen A. Schwarzman Building aka the NY Public Library.

And because Ari was "in no mood" and Vik wasn't leaving her, and Jimmy protested he was too far behind and we could just catch him up later, it was just the two of us left to shiver and peer down into the night.

As another gust of wind blows, I find myself taking cover by the library lion sculptures, heading for the one named Fortitude on the north side, less because I know which way the wind blows, but just guessing Fortitude will be more useful than the one named Patience.

THIRTEEN

It's like something out of a movie—only way less romantic. It is damp and cold and dark and incredibly foggy, and we are shivering and trying to use the backside of "Fortitude" along with each other as wind block.

And I can hear you, my friends, asking why we just didn't wait inside.

And the answer is not a) because we are gluttons for punishment nor b) because that nice, icy cold blowy, wet is great for facials. No, the answer is c) because we are morons and the library is closed.

And as we stamp and shiver in the dark, I realize Patience looks a lot less friendly after hours. Reminds me of the movie *Scrooge*; you know, when the doorknocker comes to life.

You know they also riffed on that whole Ebenezer Scrooge thing in *Scooby-Doo*. I remember the episode was "The Fright Before Christmas," but I can't remember if the door knocker came alive. This lapse I am totally and unapologetically attributing to frozen brain cell syndrome. I would bet if I were sitting someplace warm with a cup of hot chocolate I would remember.

Which is not a bad plan. I can go and find a place to buy two cups of hot chocolate and bring them back, improving both Imani's and my quality-of-life quotient immediately.

However, because the universe occasionally loves mocking me, I turn to offer to make a cocoa run, and get hit with a shot of cold wet in the face, which both glues my eyes shut and coats my square black eyeglasses in insta-shmutz. A double layer of blindness, served cold. Ugh. And as I am trying to reach a dry piece of shirt so I can wipe them open—and off—Imani shoulders right around me, peers out, pauses for just a second and then, right into my exposed ear, comes the shriek.

Imani's shriek, aside from potentially rendering me deaf, does let me connect the sound of a motorbike breaking through this frigid mist to the surprising motorbike now pulling up here. I squint, rather amazed, as said motorbike ignores the curb and pulls up right under a haloed street-light, allowing its orange-red and white striping to glisten "just so." Even to my watery eyes, peering through mist-streaked frames, to say "it made an entrance" would be a severe understatement.

This is off-the-charts noir. If Raymond Chandler himself had scripted it, it probably wouldn't have been half as brilliant.

I thankfully toss my imaginary cup of cocoa right out the imaginary window, as Imani blows right by me, racing down the steps. The leather-clad driver slams down the kickstand, hops off the bike just in time to catch the flying Imani and pull her around in an enormous, powerful swirl of a hug.

And thus it was not until after she set Imani back down that Chou Fen first took off her helmet, and I'm pretty sure my gasp would have been incredibly audible if they had been listening, which thankfully, they were not.

Imani has talked about "Fen" or "Fenny" for years. I've even seen pictures of them together in what would be about the fifth grade. And she was what one would call "adorbs," this cute, petite Chinese girl, with stick-straight, shoulder-length hair, complete with short bangs, always dressed in uniform and always charmingly having some kind of problem with it: a rolled-down sock, a button gone missing.

This person is not a Fen, and definitely not a Fenny. This

person looks like she belongs fronting FanxyRed, the Chinese boy band that is actually made up of five women. So if I were marketing them, I think I'd call them the Chinese Boi Band. But before I can finish sorting out this unexpected vision, Imani is pulling Fen over and making introductions.

"So Sid, you need to meet Ze—who you've heard me talk about for years. In our previous life, ze was better known as Chou Fen aka Fen. And now, she is well, Ze. Capital Z, small *e*."

And with that, we all kind of stand there for a brief second, no one exactly certain how best to fix that one, when Imani, to her credit, just dives back in. "Or, I guess it would be ze is now Ze. I think that is the more right way to put that.

"Ze, this is the infamous Sid. My best friend."

"Hi, Sid. It's great to meet you." Ze reached out zir hand and started laughing. I believe we all know poker face is not exactly my strong suit. I'm pretty sure Ze is now feeling awash in my bewilderment, and being kind enough not to leave it hanging there.

"Quick backstory. After Imani left school, I hung in there, somehow, for three more years. And then I couldn't take it anymore, so . . ." Ze takes a second, zir nose scrunching up as though ze is debating the best way to say this, and then with an accompanying shrug, delivers a rather peppy, "I left. And I left Fen behind with the uniform. I chose the name Ze because it still sounded Chinese, and I have fun with the redundancy." Ze's voice drops down a pitch. "Bartender, I'll have one shot of irony with a twist." And again, that big smile. "So capital Ze or small ze or they, please."

And before I can answer, Ze again extends zir hand. "And it is very nice to finally meet you. I've heard much about you over the years."

Okay. So her name was Fen. But now she's Ze. And she

uses the pronouns *ze/they*. So no *she*. No *her*. *Ze*. Or *they*. Gee, 'mani, thanks for the heads up here.

I grab the gloved hand. "It's great to finally meet you, too."

And now that we were done shivering our way through the formalities, it was time to move inside somewhere. Anywhere. I didn't really care. Coffee shop, diner, whatever either of them desired. Just as long as it came with a tenant who paid their heating bill.

Which it turns out Ze does.

And then some.

As neither Imani's allowance nor mine exactly covers taking Lyfts everywhere we'd like to go, it takes us a bit of time to arrive at the address Ze gave us, which turns out to be a four-story building in Chelsea. We race our way in, pass through the first set of doors, and before we can even look at the intercom index for a name, we are buzzed through into the foyer area, where there's a very small, unoccupied front desk counter.

"So, we're heading down there." Ze motions to a staircase behind the empty front counter. "This used to be a B and B, and my family bought it when it went on the market, partially for an investment and partially for office space."

Ze continues to chat as we follow behind, the stairwell light coming on automatically as we approach. "But there's a studio apartment down here which we keep for personal use when we're in town."

And it is suddenly incredibly surreal. This was Fenny, but now Fenny is Ze, and ze's not only here in New York, but has an apartment. And I would have yelled at Imani, but the truth is she is looking as dazed and confused as I am feeling. Compathy is us.

If Ze noticed our shared state, ze was classy enough to pay it no mind.

Wow. The downstairs door opens up to this surprisingly great space. It's basically one long room, broken visually into sections, with a small sitting area under the narrow window by the street side; a huge bookcase along one wall with a double-door closet on either side; and a small kitchen area with a table left of the entrance, which ends in another, larger bank of windows lining the back.

"Okay, so Imani sent me the picture." As we glance about, Ze begins reciting and confirming what ze knows so far. "And as you guys said, it looks like a mah-jongg tile, but it isn't one. Or at least it isn't a traditional game tile. Look, without overloading you, there are generally 144 tiles in a game. They break down into Simple tiles, which are dots, characters and bamboo; Honor tiles, which are winds and dragons; and Bonus tiles, which are flowers and seasons."

Ze pauses and motions for our jackets, which get tossed on a small table near the window. "None of these would be the picture you sent. Your picture is blurry not because of something with the screen shot, but because it's a very bad Photoshop overlay on a tile, or at least something to mimic a tile."

"But that's not particularly interesting. People like to tag all sorts of things. In this case, the message is what's very curious." Ze stops, opens the refrigerator, and pulls out a beer. "Anyone else?"

Before I can decline, I hear a delighted gasp from Imani. Ze laughs, and passes over a pastis, with a really affectionate and amused, "Some things never change." I decline the beer and the pastis. Drinking licorice is not in my wheelhouse, even though I have to say Mama did try. I do take a Coke.

Drinks now in hand, Ze picks back up. "The message is actually the Chinese characters for SOS or help."

Imani and I look over at each other. Talk about an unexpected answer.

"Basically, someone is tagging an SOS."

"You're sure."

"Positive."

And with that, the three of us just fall silent. I mean, what do you say? I look at them and say, "Okay. I'm confused. This makes even less sense now. Whoever this is already has all the toys, so why would he or she post 'help'? I mean why not just ask for it? Go into the global chat and say, hey bro, I need some help here?"

"Don't know, but there's only one way we're going to find out." Ze scoops up our jackets and tosses them over onto a coffee table. "We get ourselves online and see if we can track them down."

And with that, I reach into my bag to grab my laptop, while Ze crosses to the street side of the apartment and flings open the far closet doors, where it turns out there is a small office tucked inside, hiding a huge amount of computing equipment. There's a couple of Macs, two PCs, and in the center a gaming system. And we're not talking one of those off-the-rack-all-in-one-buy-your-own-copy-of-Word. Nope. This is custom, seriously gamer custom.

At my whistle, Ze turns back and beams. "Awesome, isn't it? Powered by a Core i7-8700K six-core processor."

"You built this?" Wowzerhole. I gape. Ze turns and boots.

"Okay. The first thing we need to do is get off the public airwaves and set up a group channel. No one is on this channel unless we agree we are inviting them in."

Smart.

"User names?"

And freeze. Personal power surge . . . engage. Face flush . . . achieved. This is *that* moment, the one where parents, teachers, and writers for teen magazines warn a person over and over about being very careful what you post. This is the moment a person should have something cool, something insanely classic. And not the now embarrassingly juvenile, teenage-brained "vixen2927. Small v."

Ze pauses. Never looks up, but I do see the slight shake in zir head. It's one I know too well. It's the one that says, "too easy, not going there."

FOURTEEN

And several hours later, I can officially declare myself a founding member of the futilitarian's club.

Imani left hours ago, right after Ze agreed, "I like your friend. She is very sweet."

That compliment followed our easy-peasy plan number one . . . fail. Which was to go online, find the user name of whoever put the tag down, and track them backward. This led us to nothing but a fake account, along with all the approval Imani needed for her to bail, leaving me here with our next plan. The evil, sadistic one where we get back to playing the game with me still no closer to leveling up than I have been for the last twenty-four hours.

Which really isn't all that long. Just long enough to determine that eighteen is not my lucky number.

During this same time, Ze spent an entire day doing who knows what and in our few hours has leveled up to twenty. Yeah. Feeling the burn.

"You know, Sid." Ze's voice interrupts my useless glaring at the screen. "In China, as in Judaism, the number eighteen is very auspicious. It is, for example, very good luck to live in a house or apartment with that number. They say you will have great success and be very prosperous."

And while talking, ze simultaneously continues to fly across the keyboard, beating back yet another virus attack. "But of course in tarot the number eighteen is associated with the moon. And the moon is weeping. And they say it is because the material is trying to destroy the spiritual."

"So," Ze pauses zir game and looks over, "before your spirit is destroyed, I suggest we stay with the combined blessings of a Jewish life and a Chinese prosperous life and get you off this level."

I am many things, but right now, proud is not one of them. Before zir offer is finished, I am offering up a Vulcan salute, rising, and then bowing with a flourish over my now vacant seat.

"It is all yours."

I go and stand kind of over Ze's shoulder, but a little ways back, trying hard to pay attention while discreetly unkinking my neck and lower back. And as I straighten back up, I get lost watching Ze's hands fly across the keyboard, seamlessly moving my avatar across the screen.

And it's a pretty intense and really awesome show. Watching Ze's fingers fly is like watching, I don't know, maybe a ballet?

No, that's not right. It's more like when you see a street group dance-off where first one guy goes and then the next guy—only in Ze's case, one guy is like the left hand and the next guy is like the right hand.

And they're amazing. They fly and then they dip and then they . . .

. . . *oh no. No. No. Hands? Really? No. No. No.* I close my eyes, squeeze my thighs, and cringe to myself. I did not just think that. That would not be the thought I am meaning to have.

Which is a problem, because it's too late. I have now had it.

And I'm not talking about some goofy movie "dance of the sensuous fingers" thing turning me on. No. It's more like a rush. Pouncing. You know, when a cat stares down its target and waits and then . . . Bam! It's all energy. And it's not a singular bam. It's rapid-fire. And with each Ze keyboard pounce, I feel it in regions I would rather not discuss.

I step back, trying to keep the sound of my breathing to myself. Inhale. Exhale. I can do this. Focus.

And I do. Staring at zir hands, I focus on the left finger, tattooed open-ended with half the Millau Viaduct Bridge. Right after Imani left and we took a break, I asked Ze about the tat.

"Ah." Ze held up zir left hand, turning it so I could see the tattooed side. "Well, the Chinese believe that each finger is a representation of the past, the present, and the future generations of you and your family. The thumb represents your parents, the index finger represents your siblings, the middle finger represents you, the ring finger represents your partner, and the pinky represents your children."

As Ze spoke, ze waggled each finger separately. When ze was finished, ze looked over to me, held up zir right hand and continued, "Okay. So now you do this with me. Start by placing your palms together as if you were praying."

Fervently hoping I have clean hands and nails, I do as ze asks, bringing them together in front of me. Having seen way too many episodes of TV shows with Chinese secondary characters, I nearly embarrass myself beyond repair by automatically assuming we are going to bow to each other like some kind of "Weedhopper and Master Po." Fortunately, I catch myself with just the smallest, telltale half-step hop.

If Ze notices, ze is kind enough to not react.

"Okay, so with your fingertips still touching, take your middle fingers and while they are touching, bend them down, until second knuckle of each middle finger is touching the other and their tips are pointing down into your palm. Now it's key to remember, the middle fingers represent you.

"So now, you're just going to let your pinkies move back. Keep everything else touching, but let the pinkies untouch each other. If you remember, the pinkies represent your children. And they can "un-touch" because children eventually leave home and go build families of their own. Which is more or less the same philosophy behind your thumbs. The thumbs represent your parents, so of course they can separate easily, because your parents are not destined to live with you forever."

At that ze pauses and smiles at me. "At least for my sake, I hope not.

"As for your index fingers, again, no resistance. The index fingers are your siblings, and they, too, will go on to live life on their own.

"This brings us to the ring finger. So, with your middle fingers still in position, try to separate your ring finger."

I attempt to do as instructed.

Ze smiles. "You see, you cannot. No matter how hard you try, they will not come apart. In Chinese folklore, this explanation is because the union between you and your partner is unbreakable, and a wedding ring worn on the ring finger represents a marriage that is meant to last forever.

"So for me, if I ever find my 'unbreakable' it will be time for my bridge to span across us both. Until then, it is incomplete."

And just as I'm thinking, or maybe not even thinking, just kind of melting, Ze continues, "or it might be because it seemed cool at the time."

And it takes a second for her words to register. And as they do, I feel my bubble burst. Apparently so could Ze, who looks at me and laughs. "Uh oh. Another born romantic I have now horrified."

And my friends, in case you find it useful to know, the folklore is true. It is an ancient Chinese belief.

Anatomically however, I can actually tell you how this phenomenon works. We have a common muscle called extensor digitorum that has little connectors between the tendons that go to the backs of each finger that allow them to extend all the way. The thumb is separate, but in addition to this muscle, the pinky has a second muscle called extensor digiti minimi and the pointer has a second muscle called extensor indicis. When you bend the middle fingers, you fix the tendons of the extensor digitorum, and without a second muscle to assist it your ring finger is stuck.

As is my brain.

Which is how I got here. Dazed, confused, aroused. And way too tired to have any rational thoughts left.

Which is okay, because apparently I didn't need any, because that way, they didn't keep me awake.

And I know this because I am woken up by the sound of *tap, tap, tap,* which I slowly realize is someone knocking on a window, and they are calling out for Ze, which jerks me wide awake. Ze. Heart palpitations begin. Ze. Quick glance around, apparently still in the closet, gaming. Wow.

It seems I fell asleep on the couch outside of the closet, somewhere in the middle of the night. The good news is I had the forethought to text the parental unit that Imani and I were at Fenny's, so I wouldn't be killed. (Hey, explaining it was just me and Fenny, who is now Ze, is a way bigger story than a text would have handled.) The bad news is that Ze is now out of the closet and opening the door to one of the most beautiful, hippest women I've ever seen outside of the movies, and I am stumbling upward, barefoot, wearing unquestionably slept-in clothes, having bed-head hair sticking out sideways, and, oh yeah, a wee bit of crusty drool stuck on the side of my mouth.

Lovely.

She tilts her impossibly hip, multi-braided head and looks me up and down with these huge eyes. It occurs to me she is going for the Chinese hip-hop artist, Vava, look, and she's nailing it, but in a really cold, calculated way. She turns from me to Ze, her eyebrow raised in question.

I should mention, thankfully, that Ze looks exactly like I left zir last night. Apparently ze never went to bed.

"Oh hey." Ze turns to make introductions. "Babe, this is Sid. She's a friend of Imani's, you know, who I went to school with back in the day. Anyway, they have a problem I'm trying to help them with.

"Sid, this is my girlfriend, Xing."

The good news is the eyebrow lowers as I give my little grin and wave. The bad news is I know instinctively she is the wrong person and I hate her. I am sensing we both know this is already mutual . . .

. . . but irrelevant. I am sized up and quickly dismissed as Xing turns back to Ze, and with a pout says, "Babe, aren't we going this morning?"

Ze looks at her and then blinks. "Ah shit.

"Okay. Give me two minutes to get changed, and we go." And as Ze crosses to the other closet, ze calls back, "Hey Sid, I'm sorry. We have to get over to Brooklyn for a parkour competition."

And I'm thinking hard, plowing deep in the recesses . . . Parkour? Oh yeah, parkour is that thing where people run up the sides of buildings and leapfrog fences and, I dunno, jump from one city rooftop across to another, apparently for fun. Yep. Check. That's the one. That's parkour. And I'm thinking, *really, why?*

A thought that must have been really easy to read, because I look up to see cutesy head-tilt smirking at me. "Ze's going to world's this year, you know." It's less sharing than sneering. Or maybe gloating.

Either way, before I can think to answer, Ze snorts as ze jumps back out of the closet, now wearing sweats and a black muscle tee, which fit ridiculously well. "Love you, babe, but not too sure about that one." Ze's headshake is affectionate as ze gives a playful laugh, and then turns back to me, conspiratorially. "I think the only way I ever go to world's is as a fan, but I have fun."

"Look, Sid." Ze's voice drops, signals new topic. "I'm really sorry I completely forgot about this. I didn't find our phantom friend last night, but I promise I will continue the search later. But now, if you'd like, you are welcome to come with us."

The bad news here is twofold: 1) parkour and 2) because Xing is behind Ze, only I can see the death glare pointing directly at me.

"Me? Thank you. Uhm, no can do." And now I am fumbling every which way, verbally, physically. "You know, late night last night. I gotta get home, catch up before school."

Oh yes, my peeps. You know it. Suave Sid strikes again.

I stumble out, hit the sidewalk, and just to rub it all in, have an old treppenwitz moment. You know, the one where your witty retort is just one moment too late. Parkour? Me? Love to, but I'm sorry, I've already committed to running with the bulls.

Big sigh. Another day-late, dollar-short moment.

FIFTEEN

I point my still-tripping-over-my-two-left-feet-exiting-the-apartment body toward home with the intention of checking in with the parental unit, maybe doing some schoolwork, and then with whatever time was left returning to the hunt.

I begin walking when a particular ping lets me know I have a DM on my twitter. It's Dan, telling me he has nothing to tell me. Yeah, I am not surprised. That kind of morning.

But I DM back, giving him my best graciousness. Hey, you never know. And now, being as I am in Chelsea, I think I should maybe stroll along the High Line for at least a few blocks, which lets my mind roam, and leads me back to thinking about last night. And fascination . . .

So I sit down on one of my benches. Versus infatuation.

And then I text the parental unit to say all is good, be home in a few hours, and then . . . then I reach a decision and ping Ari.

An hour or so later, this is where she finds me, occupying my usual High Line bench, affectionately known as "my office." Part of me thinks I need to get less predictable, but mostly I am grateful it's not raining so I don't have to think about a different place.

And for the next few minutes we just sit there, side by side, sharing my bench, staring out, watching the world walk by. I watch a small cluster of clouds race across the sky, apparently having places to go, people to rain on.

We hang for what seems like forever, but is most likely five minutes, looking across the way and taking in the city. All those windows, all with people behind them. I wonder sometimes what they're like. The people, not the windows. I read a book once where the train stops outside this girl's window. And she sees a girl her age staring back. I don't really remember too much else, other than it was an el train.

Sometimes I wonder if maybe there's a girl out there looking at me, only I can't see her.

Exhale. Big sigh.

It's time. I screw up my courage and turn to Ari. "How do you know if you're attracted to someone?"

Ari doesn't say anything. But she does turn and look straight at me. Waiting. Apparently for me to continue.

This is like ripping off a Band-Aid. However much it hurts, do it fast.

"I don't mean it that way exactly. I mean, what if you think you might have feelings for someone but they aren't the someone you think you should have feelings for?" And as soon as I rush the last of that thought out, I find a study of my knuckles is desperately needed. "I mean maybe they're not feelings. Well, of course they're feelings but maybe they're not *those* kinds of feelings."

"Hey Sid?"

I take a brief second before I peer up. "Yeah?"

Ari leans over and gently pushes my hair down. Without product it has a mind of its own. "This will be a lot easier if we just use proper nouns."

Nouns? I mull that over. Nouns could be good.

"I'm going to guess our topic is Fenny slash Ze."

And just like that, it's out there. And I'm a rubber band ball of emotions, embarrassed, thankful she said it, really super thankful she already knows about the Ze of it all, ashamed I need this, and incredibly afraid that if I bounce and hit a band the wrong way, it will snap.

"Your challenge, Sid, is that you are a sapiosexual." And

with that pronouncement my head jerks up. "The issue is, you think brains are sexy. Which for the record, I concur."

Ari pauses, watching me closely. "And do not be looking at me that way. We do, you know, go to the same school. I, too, can be very vocab forward."

I tip my imaginary hat and think, *touché*, but say nothing. Perhaps because I am too busy thinking, *Brains? Brains are sexy. But so are fingers? Brains, fingers? Who knew? I didn't. I so did not know fingers could be so . . . maybe I should check out typists? Think about all the finger workouts they get.*

Unaware of my drifting, Ari returns to her Sid diagnosis mode, which wisely interrupts my inner voice.

"And it is better than being, what's the word?" Ari looks at me expectantly.

And although I'm good, I need a bit more than that.

"You know, the one for being attracted to fools?"

"Insipiosexual?"

"That's it. Thank you. And no. No I don't really see you as someone who would be attracted to a fool. But then again . . ." Ari's face breaks into a small teasing smile, accompanied by a small shoulder shove, ". . . they do say love is blind."

"Ari, do you know the rest of that quote?" My question is redundant, so I don't bother to wait for an answer. "And lovers do not see the follies that they themselves commit."

And if we're gonna sit here and quote Shakespeare, here's my rub. My problem is there is no "they." There is only an I. I do not see the follies that I myself commit.

"Aw, Sid," Ari's arm snakes over my shoulder, "listen to Doctor Ari. You, my friend, are just having a bout of perfectionist paralysis. You take an idea, create everything in your head, and then you expect it to follow precisely the way you planned it in life. This won't happen.

"And you know, Sid," Ari pushes away, once again waiting to catch my eye, "even if this is a folly. A folly or two won't kill you."

And it never ceases to fascinate me. Even when she's being my friend, she always wraps her spiel up in such a way that she is doing that cat paw/lick thing.

We continue to just hang out and pass the afternoon, sitting on the bench, watching people go by, letting the litany of languages, the lilting of accents, and the variety of customs wash over us, their passing patter as much a part of our city as Lady Liberty herself. Occasionally we become invested enough in a passerby or two to deem them worthy of a thumbs up, but more routinely only breaking our silence to deliver the snarkiest of observations.

And betwixt and between, we chat.

"Hey, Sid?" Ari breaks the silence. "Why me?"

And I can hear the second part of that question, the part she isn't giving voice to. "I would have thought you would have called Imani?"

And I have to think on this before I answer. I watch a Hasidic family cross in front of us, the little boys with their long peyes, laughing and running. Ari's right. If you were guessing, you'd assume Imani is who I would have called. And yet I didn't. But I know why.

It's because, at least to me, Ari is way more sophisticated about these things than Imani. Not sophisticated in knowing more gay people or nonbinary people or pangender people, but it's just kind of like she's just more sexually advanced or maybe astute or maybe just out there. I do know I'm not sure how best to say this without it sounding like I'm making it a bad thing or something.

"I don't know." I stop and think, trying to find words that are both honest and nonjudgmental. "I think maybe because you're in control of who you are. You own you."

And I know that's true, even if it's not all of the truth. Ari is defiantly Ari. And that's the piece I trust about her.

Instead of a solemn, "I get it" or "Thank you," I am taken aback by the shlaughter aka shout of laughter that bursts from her. Not the kind of laughing between friends or at a joke, but rather that short, mean kind of laughter that brings me up short.

"Hey, Sid." Ari stands up, crosses to the other side of the path, and then walks back slowly, a kind of bitter amusement on her face. She stops in front of me, suddenly towering. "I'm going to share one last secret with you. None of us is in control of who we are. That's the great cosmic fuster cluck."

Ari looks at me and seems to come to some kind of decision. But she doesn't sit down. She motions to me, and we cross to the other side and lean against the rail, looking over the city. "You know how you always ask, why Vik?"

All of a sudden, with the sharpest of screaming clarity, it crosses my mind I don't really want to know. That it's not going to be a funny, flirty story.

But I don't reach out to stop her.

"Here's why. I was raped by my stepfather." Ari turns sideways, looking directly to me. "It was my eleventh birthday present." Her voice never changes. She could be telling a stranger to take a left at the corner. And that's the giveaway. "It took my mother a full year to throw him out."

Ari pushes herself back, getting a bit of physical distance from both me and the rail. "So to say it left me with issues would be an understatement. And, as I know you know," Ari suddenly gives off her characteristic smile and head toss, "I drank too much and I partied too much and I screwed around way too much."

As she's talking, and acknowledging how I knew her then, I realize I have kind of forgotten all about that. I mean it wasn't so long ago she was all that, but now she's just my friend.

"And then I wound up in Carson's chemistry class and I was assigned Vik as my partner." Ari laughs, lost in that moment. And I'm happy because I know that moment is happier for her. "And god, he had that terrible emo flap and he was such a geek, but you know, Sid, he thought I was the bomb. And not in some cheap, 'I hear she'll put out' way, but as in, I was the girl just beyond his reach."

"And one day, Sid, I actually asked him out, because I wanted to be," Ari pauses for just a second, not looking at me, searching for something. "No, that's not quite right," she amends herself. "It's because I needed to be, the girl he saw."

Even though Ari falls silent, I don't say anything, because I somehow don't think she is finished. And I am right. She isn't. But her finish, I think, is less for me than for her.

"And you know what, Sid?" A small grin begins to break through. "Now there are some days, actually a lot of days, I truly am that girl."

With that, we both fall silent again. I'm kind of awestruck. I never thought any of that. In my mind I always knew exactly why Vik dated Ari. Only now it turns out I never really did know any of it.

Slowly we turn, making our way along, until we find ourselves by the waterfront, heading down to grab a slice.

"So, Sid, what's with you and Mae Ann and Mae Lee?"

Now I could pretend I don't know what she's talking about, but that would be incredibly uncool at this point in our day. I resort to a shrug, leaving the interpretation of said gesture wide open. Could mean, I dunno what you're talking about or could mean, I dunno what's with it? Noncommittal, not to mention nonverbal, seems my wisest choice of action.

"You know their real story, don't you?"

"You mean, the whole their-mother-died thing and Grandma came over . . .yeah."

"Yeah, well, it wasn't quite like that. When they tell it or we hear it or whatever, it's kind of heroic sounding. But actually their mother committed suicide. She climbed into their crib with them. And when they found her, they were on either side of her, wet diapers and crying. They say they don't remember that part, but they do know their dad didn't even want to look at them. So her mother came over from

China and did all the proper things, but basically hated their dad for taking her daughter away, and the two of them, because they replaced her daughter. So all they were left with was each other."

And I don't think I said it out loud, but I know I did manage to stop mid-pizza bite, dripping both sauce and cheese onto my chin, which one could translate as, "no way, and you know this how?"

"I was out shopping. And I ran into them. They were looking at a wall where someone had done those tiles with single Chinese symbols on them for like, luck or hope. And they weren't capable of reading them. And they're kind of basic." Ari scrunches her nose. "Or at least they should be."

Ari pauses, assessing me somehow, searching me for an answer, only I don't know the question.

"And I guess I'm telling you all this because maybe if you have some context, you can see a few things better. Like why they are so attached." Ari once again pauses, still calculating something. "And Sid, maybe if you see them better, you'll also see them differently. Like maybe you'll see why Mae Ann chose to stay on the coding team?"

I don't know exactly what she is trying to tell me, but I am too over the day to ask, and honestly not particularly interested. The sun is sinking, and it's getting exponentially colder. And I look at Ari, backlit, wind blowing through her hair, watching as it lifts, the strands separating and all the colors shimmering—the blond with the pinks, blue, purple and, ooohhh, a hint of green . . .

And you know, I don't know if I get it. I do know I get that it's different. I get that Ze is different, and I get that Ari is different, and I get that we're all doing the best we can. But I don't know if I get what Ari thinks I do.

"Hey Ari?" I know we're about to head our own ways, but I have one last question for her. "Did you ever read *The Wizard of Oz* books . . . you know, *The Road to Oz* and so on?"

"Nope."

"Well there's a character in them. Her name's Polychrome. And at one point, she says to Dorothy, 'You have some queer friends, Dorothy.'" And I pause for a moment before I finish, "To which Dorothy answers, 'The queerness doesn't matter, so long as they're friends.'"

And we both pause for another minute. Watching the world go by. Watching Ari's rainbow hair blow around. "Thanks, Ari."

SIXTEEN

And now I do finally head home, once again filled with great intentions. The day with Ari has left me in an oddly mellow and surprisingly sanguine mood about everything. I let myself in, welcoming the smells from the kitchen, planning to just enjoy a lovely familial dinner and then dedicate some time to catching up on my tonnage of neglected homework.

It begins just as I envisioned it. Yes, there was a bit of a raised eyebrow from Mom, but since I had texted and made it home early enough not only to eat, but to actually help prep, it was not the hairy eyeball of death, just the quirked is-everything-okay-I-am-keeping-my-eye-on-you one, which is manageable.

And Dad and I stand together, chopping vegetables for the salad, which really means I chop vegetables while he takes turns annoying Mom and amusing me with bad singing impressions, until Jean comes home carrying a loaf of French bread and then, *voila*, here we are, happily dining on pasta, salad, a little garlic bread, indulging in a little chit, a little chat.

Jean complains about a math exam, and then Dad tells some long-winded story about his latest star sighting, one that involves Neil deGrasse Tyson crashing his lunch and therefore, "because you are known by the company you keep," having people falling all over his feet. And somehow he manages to tie up this story by sharing his version of some inverted Aesop-type moral, in case we needed help. "And you know, it would be nice to get a little more feet falling from my family."

For the record, there are no takers for this undisguised, pathetic attempt to bait us. There is, however, the trio of jeer, snort, and scoff.

It's my night for clearing the table and washing the dishes, which is really about rinsing them off and stacking them in the dishwasher, because my Mama is a member of the you-wash-the-dishes-before-the-dishwasher-washes-them club. So I begin as everyone else heads off on their own ways.

I actually don't mind dishwashing night because the quiet combined with monotony does occasionally provide me with a good use of head-clearing time, and sometimes inspiration will strike.

Which is why I absurdly thought I might think about the paper I am theoretically writing on Anne Brönte's *The Tenant of Wildfell Hall*, or for that matter even replaying my conversations with Ari, but no. Instead I start mulling about the game, wondering if the reason I can't uncover what's going on is because I am missing the obvious?

All this mulling has the unfortunate side effect of leaving my defenses wide open for attack when Mom strolls into the kitchen, finds me standing here, silently pondering, *why is it the only times we have found Tile-Boy he is near the same cave?*, staring off into space, with a wet plate in my hand and the water running. She reaches around my unseeing self and turns the water off, then leans against the sink, studying me.

Busted. Am I. And if you don't know, an apartment kitchen is incredibly tiny, but highly efficient. And when Mama is on the hunt, the kitchen is a perfect trap. I honestly don't think it's mere coincidence she just happened around the corner. I think she was lying in wait. She is the master of the art of waiting. She is also the master of the cheap trick. I, sadly, am the master of folding. Like a cheap suit.

As she gently removes the suspended-in-air plate, she says, "Ah Sidonie, *tu faire des châteaux en Espagne.*"

Which is a French idiom for you are building castles in the air. However, it is mom-speak for "spill it."

"*Ce n'est rien*, Mama." I shrug, force a half smile. "It's nothing."

She does not reply, but her body slightly adjusts, so now her hip moves against the counter, while the arms cross. This is the not quite annoyed, but inviting me to speak stance.

"No. Really." And I am scrambling through my cranial rolodex to find an adequate response, one that will be credible and still not give away too much. Or at least more than I want. "I mean, I told you I was with Imani and her old school chum, Fenny, right?"

Pause for the nod.

"Well, Imani never told me that Fenny is now Ze, so I was kind of surprised by all that and just thinking about it."

And while this wasn't what I was actually thinking about, it isn't really a lie either. I mean it has been on my mind. Mostly because if I think about it, I just don't get why Imani never said anything. I mean it's not something I would have ever judged. Which of and by itself could mean it was something Imani was judging. Or maybe something she didn't want me to know. But why? Or is it, why not?

"And how does Fenny being Ze make you feel?"

Like I am super thankful I spent the afternoon with Ari. And also oddly thankful Mom cut to the chase. No tiptoeing around, asking for more details. Just a direct question aimed right at the heart of the matter. "No. I mean, it's all good. Ze seems really cool. It was just kind of, well, surprising, you know?" Wow, Sid, could you sound any more pathetic if you tried? At least I didn't wince.

Or maybe I did.

Mom raises her right arm and kind of lays her chin on her fist, hooks her right index finger around her lips and looks at me. I think she is about to say something, but instead she lowers her hand, tuts to herself, and turns to go.

But then, just as I think I can relax, exhale, with one final head quirk, she reaches back out to pick my chin up. Even as I lift my eyes to meet hers, I am fighting, trying to keep them from being either defiant or smug or caught out, or anything that she can somehow read.

And I try to distract my brain by thinking I will be inscrutable. Okay, yeah, not so much.

Enigmatic. I wish.

Incomprehensible. That one might work. I will try and maintain incomprehensible.

She lets go of my chin and leaves me with one parting thought, "Ah, Sidonie, why are we going to have to do this the hard way?"

And I do wonder for just a millisecond if she means the story of Ze or the story I am not telling. Then I wonder, which one do I mean?

SEVENTEEN

"I've got it."

Because we are in the library, I am required to hiss my words, which is kind of annoying. But at least it's not as bad a place for a meet-up as it used to be, which is great, 'cause the weather outside sucks this morning. But ever since our Battle-Axe-of-Books, Mrs. Stewart, took a leave of absence, and our replacement librarian arrived, complete with a super-cool, blue-tipped undercut fade, and at least a half dozen earrings posted through the ear on the shaved side of her head, the library has acquired a whole new vibe.

But still not one that says, don't mind me, go ahead and shout. So, I first eye-checked everyone, making sure I had their complete and undivided attention, which allowed me, despite my having to hiss, to winningly convey an appropriate sense of triumph.

Self-satisfied, I sit back.

"Uhm, Sid," Vikram looks across at me and plasters a smile on his face, "as much as I am sure you are completely right about this new theory of yours, you do know we have a robot to build."

The theory he is referring to would be the one I finally solidified last night by going back to the obvious. Only one high-level player got ripped off. And the rip-off artist, holding that player's stuff, keeps hanging about, yet the only thing we really know about him is he has crafted a mahjongg tile that begs for help in Chinese.

"I got here by just laying out and staying with what we actually know." I focus directly at Vikram. "The old KISS, or keep it simple, stupid. If you don't extrapolate or theorize anything, the linear train leads you to, *Hey Vik, now that I have your attention, I need help.*

"Which, given he has all your stuff, would really seem to mean, hey Vik, I need *your* help."

I let my eyes roam about again, giving him time to think this through as I continue. "So yes. I think this is actually personal. I think tile-boy isn't answering us because he needs Vik for some reason. And the problem is, since tile-boy has all your stuff, we can't rely on getting you through the game without wasting a lot of time. And even if we could, what would that actually change other than you could get inside the cave?"

I glance to the wall clock. Twelve minutes until the first bell.

"So I think we shortcut this by getting ourselves into the cave, and leaving a message. Something along the lines of, if he wants to meet you, you will be in the emergency room tomorrow at ten."

I hear Imani laugh, but it's actually Ari who asks, "Really, Sid? The emergency room? Again?"

Less than ten minutes left, but I slow down long enough to give a laugh, and answer. "Funny one, Ari. It's one of the dungeons. In this particular game, to gain access to this dungeon, you have to be a level twenty or higher, which Vik, Jimmy, Ze and yes, even me, are. Vik doesn't need to be playing to hang out there, we only need his ranking, so his not having antidotes or power-ups or whatever won't matter. We just cruise in, hang and wait."

Jimmy is doing his I'm-just-evaluating-chair-tipping-thing, which stops as he rocks forward. "And you figured all this how?"

The correct answer would be this all came to me last

night, right after Mom's question about "doing" this the hard way echoed in my head for a good fifteen minutes.

Somehow, in the middle of spinning my story I'd actually forgotten that I was using Ze as a cover story for an important question I didn't want to answer. Ironically my cover story *un*covered a voice telling me that I am actually annoyed or perturbed, or maybe just a bit hurt, over now feeling set up.

So I kept turning the silence of Imani over in my mind repeatedly, asking myself why, if not before, then at least when we were standing there freezing our derrières off, she didn't say anything about Fenny now being Ze. Was it about me? Was it about her? Was it about Ze?

And this kept going on a loop right up until it occurred to me I didn't need to do this the hard, introspective way. I could just call her or text her, or wait until tomorrow, definitely the better choice, and just ask her if never having mentioned the whole Fenny-is-now-Ze thing was somehow personal . . . and then . . . it just kind of flipped like a light switch and I had it.

The answer to our question is "personal." As in, yes, it is *personal*. Not, just "personal" regarding Imani, but personal regarding the thief-in-the-game answer as well.

Thus, because it would be way too long and I have no time, I don't bother with Jimmy's question and continue my theory. "I mean, what if we just accept, for just a minute here, that tile-boy is trying to tell us something." And I sit up higher, crossing one leg under me, as I verbally process this out. "Then the question becomes tell us what, right?"

"I compiled all the clues I could find, beginning with the day Vik was ripped off. Now, whoever this is, still appears to be playing a zero sum game. Not selling. Not profiting. Not even engaging in spite of their call for help.

"But yet," and my hands thrust outward, "he's still there." My gestures get both larger and more pointed as I get into

109

it. "And only ever spotted in the one of the three caves that lets you leave a signature, which only lasts until the next person comes in."

It's a tough crowd, but none tougher than Vik, who is still a tad touchy when the *Contagion* hunt comes up, and the only one among us who really knows gaming. As I gesture larger, he seems to shrink an inch further away. But I am not going to be intimidated.

"The only time he goes into the cave is after anyone else gets in. All he does is erase their name and put his same tile back up. It's as though he is waiting for something, but . . ." I pause. I know this is all a bit loose and wonky, but I also know it's pretty darn close. To quote the suddenly omnipresent, and omniscient, Dr. Woodie, overselling here isn't going to help me.

Big raspberry.

Followed by first bell ringing.

Argh. I run my hand through my hair, quickly check each of them. "Look." I try to work this through, pleading with them to follow along, maybe even take a bit of the lead. "I don't know it all exactly, but it's as though he can't let his tile fall into the wrong hands somehow. Kind of like if this was a *Scooby* episode, the clue would be hidden in, I don't know, disappearing ink."

And by now, we are all rising and I start pacing as I talk, slowing their exit while trying to find the piece I know is missing. "But even if the ink is disappearing, there still is a clue. Which, to me means, whoever he is, he is somehow deliberately trying to communicate something, even as he's hiding it from," I pause, "the wrong hands."

And now I stop, look at everyone. See if any of this has made any impression. But no one is jumping on my bandwagon.

Finally, Imani breaks the silence. "What makes it a he?"

Well that one wasn't on my list of questions. Kind of weird that's what she picked up out of all that. I want to say,

110

got gender on your mind, Imani? But I don't. Mostly because if she does, I can't say as I really blame her. And also, well, because, maybe she doesn't and maybe it's just me. Maybe I'm the one with gender on my mind.

So I mumble back, "Sorry. Nothing. It was generic speak. I don't know. That it's a he. I mean that's what I don't know."

"Look, Sid," Jimmy wades in, "you," he pauses to amend, "*we*, know nothing. We don't even know for certain that whoever this is speaks either English or Chinese. The tile is a pretty crude overlay. It could have come from anywhere."

Which is absolutely true. But I don't think so. So I just stand here, waiting, until Jimmy sighs. "Okay, we have," he checks his watch, "two minutes left. So what's your thinking?"

Thank you, Mr. Flynn. Still my wingman.

"So glad you asked." I shoot him a grin, but keep talking. "I'm thinking whoever he, or she, is wants something, but for some reason won't use the global chat. So I think we see if said person will meet us in a dungeon."

"Really?" Vik jumps back into the conversation. "And how exactly do you think we manage that?"

And there it is. The moment I have been praying for, the one when someone tees up my question for me. They're thinking they've got you, but it's that exhilarating rush knowing you really just got them. I try not to be too gleeful.

"We set up a raiding party, and we get Ze into the cave. And Ze goes in and leaves behind a signature that gives Vik's game name, time, and place in both Chinese and English."

And with that I wait. The clock tick is practically jumping off the wall into my face, but I wait.

Vik nods first, and with that we all agree, leaving us with only one problem. And as much as I'd like to shrug *don't bore me with the details*, that unfortunately is not an option.

You see, we aren't enough people to mount a raiding

party. *We* would be Ze, Jimmy and me. If you take Ze away, because Ze has to be poised to get inside, that leaves me and Jimmy, with only one of us having any kind of potential raiding skills. It's a dilemma. But one, the ringing bell shrills, that will have to wait.

Class calls. I make my way down the hallway, avoiding backpacks and late arrivers, heading to my first class. All the while planning how to do this. So I know, as much as I hate this idea, Jean is actually a really good gamer and I can get him and his moron best friend, Aaron, up to speed, which would at least qualify us to be a very minimal raiding party, with four on the corners, and a shot at approaching this with some strategic thinking. And if I threaten them with death, or worse, they will keep their mouths shut.

And thus, head still in my mission, I swagger into AP Calc, where I find Scott and Mae Ann, already there and scarily chatting away, deep in the throes of what is apparently their topic of the day: Which role featured the most kick-ass Charlize Theron? Cipher, Furiosa or Lorraine?

"Hey guys." I grab the chair in front of them and turn around. "I hate to interrupt this incredibly important, and honestly on another day brilliant, discussion, but Mae Ann, I need you for something," which I guess, judging from the reaction from both Mae Ann and Scott, isn't often on my list of things I say. "I mean, if you're up for it?"

The smile is instant, broad, and suspiciously predatory, leaving me feeling uncomfortably like I just became the whipped cream for her dessert.

SFS! Sudden Flashback Syndrome. Ari, over a slice, *maybe you'll see why Mae Ann chose to stay on the coding team.* OMG. It was a warning. Or at least it should have been. If I'd been paying any attention.

Mae Ann emits some kind of a *squee*—and let me just say, I am no fan of the squee. I do manage to notice her fingers. They're definitely on the stubby side. And at least two of her nails are chipped.

I am not too sure if that means anything, but I am pretty sure it means something that I noticed. I'm also pretty sure my instant heebie-jeebies mean I am so going to regret this.

And just like that, *poof*, swagger is gone. I turn forward and slink down low into the hard-backed chair.

EIGHTEEN

It's now eight o'clock on Friday night and we are gathered at Ze's place in Chelsea. For the good and the bad of it, we are going to attempt this. Ze and Jimmy have been literally closeted away, plotting a strategy for over an hour, but there's no point hurrying them.

The three of us, Jean, Aaron and Mae Ann, are also present and waiting. I am happy to report there is no sign of Xing. Unfortunately, Vikram is with Marcus and Imani, finalizing the scale set piece for tomorrow's test runs, wherein our bots need to get into position and scale the wall. It's one of the trickiest parts. Scott is covering, but I'm sure I will have lots of recoding tomorrow. Ugh.

I'm not sure where Ari is, but since she can't game it's reasonably irrelevant, so we are our own slim crew with a very narrow window to get past the virus and into the cave.

And even though we make, at best, a very minimal raiding party, and Ze's apartment is, by NYC standards, an incredibly spacious studio, it is becoming increasingly oppressive for me.

"Lah Sid," Mae Ann giggles, scrunching her whole body, from her nose to her toes, including her shoulders, "this is so great. So exciting."

Need I say more? It's a simper-fest. More air sucks out. I try not to cringe.

Oh irony, how bitter you are. Mae Ann is right, this should be. Exciting, that is. It should be intense and awe-

114

some and huddle-worthy. And maybe for everyone else it is, but for me, not so much. I have detested the twincesses since their third grade arrival, and I was right then, and I am right now, and I don't care about their sad story, and I don't care about Ari's nudging, but for now, it's too late. I am trapped in twincess hell. At least until we break Ze through the plague-guarded cave entrance.

I manage a half grin, before repositioning my chair so she can't get any closer. I'm not risking that.

"Okay." Ze makes zir way out of the closet, followed by Jimmy. Everyone immediately listens up. "It's time."

"Here's the plan." Jimmy crosses to the table under the front window, motions me out of my chair, which he immediately moves so everyone can see over his shoulders, opens his tablet and starts *x*'ing and *o*'ing.

"We figured out which items will give us the best chance to succeed. In its most basic sense, we are going to execute a kind of end-around. Sid, you and Mae Ann are the front line. You two have to engage the contagion, bringing enough fire, and taking enough fire, to hold it on the front line." Jimmy draws four rows of *o*'s against two *x*'s, which represent the two of us. "You will get all our available tranq guns, anesthesia loads, and sedation stun grenades. Use them all. You have to slow it down.

"Now, Aaron and Jean, your job is to come up, take what they are holding, and string it out, weakening the center. You're each going to have a share of the antitoxins. Since we don't know what's coming at us, it's a guess as to whose potion will let them survive longer. The odds are, neither is really the right one, but they should buy a couple of extra beats, so once Sid and Mae Ann slow it, everything else has to move incredibly fast." Jimmy quickly draws two *x*'s, one on the outside of each of our *x*'s, and then from there each one gets an arrow extending out, demonstrating their route.

With this, Jimmy takes a quick pause to make sure we are all still with him. At our nods, he continues. "Okay, now

Ze is going to come from the far side, crossing behind all this, where ze will find me, holding the last payload, our shield wall. I will pass it to Ze, and then dive straight through what should now be our weakened middle, clearing the way for Ze to make a break."

So Ze's x comes from behind where Jean is, the arrow extends half wayacross, until it is behind my x, where another x, which is Jimmy, awaits. Then from Jimmy's x, two lines crash through right between Mae Ann and myself, and through the o's to the cave. "Between our damage to their line, and the shield wall, Ze should be able to get in."

"Okay everyone." Ze walks into the middle of the room, bumps zir fists together and then splays them back *à la* an explosion. "It's showtime." Ze looks down at zir watch. "We go in two minutes."

Before I can get to my screen, I see Mae Ann tossing me another scrunchy, lip-purse-y grin thing, and I take a minute to remind myself that her getting killed by whatever plague is coming at us, or by me, won't actually help our goal.

So instead, I take a deep breath, and it's time.

We're off and moving through the worlds. Mae Ann finds me, and as we make our approach, we move slowly, steadily, feeling our way, carefully carving out a path to the cave. Deep olive green and purple mists begin to stir and rise up from the long, uninhabited meadow, standing between here and there.

The closer we get, the faster the swirl; the faster the swirl, the more force they exert, challenging our ability to withstand them. At some point, as they spin, they begin coughing out gobs of viral goo. As we inch closer in, the cough picks up a violent streak, transforming into hacking puke. A chunk of puce vomits past us, followed by a ribbon of chartreuse.

Even in the midst of this chaos, I can hear my devil's advocate brain asking, "why would anyone play this game?"

Mae Ann and I try to hold our line, shooting antitoxins and tranqs back at the venom, attempting to minimize its ferocity, while ducking the viral hits and somehow not ceding our position.

I can hear Jimmy from the recesses of the closet calling out, "more left, Sid" and "Okay, Mae Ann, you got this."

As we hang in, suddenly Jimmy yells, "Now Aaron, Jean. Go, go, go."

And with that they are in here and spreading the virus out. And they are good. I can actually see the aggressive middle chunk thinning, almost like a fire is burning through its middle and eating fuel sideways.

Suddenly an orb of infection hurls from beyond the front line.

It hits Mae Ann dead on, not killing her outright, but causing her to drop back.

"Don't stop, Sid." Jimmy yells. "Ze and I are going now. Mae Ann, regroup and head toward Jean. Let's pull as much of the virus that way as we can. No, Aaron, not you. You have to hold your end!"

I lob three grenades, trying to daze the center.

Jimmy continues barking directions, and faster than I could imagine ever playing, he sweeps by me, Ze on his tail, already having executed the end around and going in. As I watch, Jimmy is surrounded by the attack, letting Ze push through with the shield wall engaged.

"And I am in."

And with that, we all rush the closet.

Triumphantly in the cave, Ze adds the signature we built on our own fake mah-jongg tile: Sunday. 3:00P. ER. Vik. Day. Time. Location. Vik.

While she is signing, we're all high-fiving and cheering and then, well, then it happens. Mae Ann throws her arms around me and says, "Lah Sid, this is so cool."

Freeze.

Whoa.

And while the would-be, might-be, but definitely not tonight, grown-up part of me knows I need to deal with this, I instead survive until I can make my way home, the whole way convincing myself this is no big deal. Telling myself over and over, we were just all caught up in the high. It's a perfectly normal part of being in the moment.

I also ignore the seven different texts she sends.

And I'm okay with all this, because Sunday at 3 p.m. we are all due back at Ze's, and then we will solve this mystery and everything can just return to normal. So it's not like I'm trying to do a friendly fade, or going ghost, or something. I mean I am going to see her in another day. All I have to do is not surface until then.

Yeah, so sometimes I suck. And sometimes I hate my life. That's probably a good, normal thing, practiced by zillions of people all over the world.

So I'm definitely not going to obsess about this. No. I'm going to practice the art of denial. During which time, I am going to write my English paper.

Come on, we're only talking about one day. Until Sunday.

Just one more day. Even if that day feels like a week. Or a month.

But I make it. And so does everyone else, including the star of our show, Vik, as well as Ari and Imani. Thankfully, even Mae Ann was smart enough to keep her distance and just let me be.

Because now is so not the time for drama. You know, we're all a bit on edge. Even as we are waiting, we're all keeping an eye on any activity in the dungeon. So while there's lots of checking our phones, getting up, moving around, grabbing a soda, and eating things with sugar—lots of sugar—there's truly virtually no talking.

And finally the appointed time comes. Nothing. And then the appointed time goes. Nothing.

A huge no-show.

And as we realize he's not coming, we all try to bolster each other with about a hundred reasons why. Maybe he isn't in the same time zone so he didn't know when our three o'clock was. Maybe he thought it was three o'clock in the morning. Maybe he just never got back to the cave to see it.

But none of it really matters. We are nowhere. Again.

Maybe we are even worse than nowhere. For the first time I have to give credence to the idea that we are victims of some psycho dude's game. But I didn't buy that then, and I don't believe it now.

I look up, checking out the room. We are the perfect picture, dictionary definition of crestfallen. Although I have to say I prefer woebegone.

Jimmy finally stands up, shrugs, and reaches for his backpack. "I'm really sorry, Sid. We gave it the best we could."

And right behind him, Vik comes over. "Thanks for trying, Sid. I really do appreciate it."

And with hugs from Imani and Ari, who thankfully takes Mae Ann with her, the apartment empties. Until there is just me and Ze. And then Ze turns to me. "I'll keep an eye out; you never know."

And just like that, it's over.

NINETEEN

And I was pretty devastated. I stayed up half the night, trying to figure out how I could have miscalculated. And yet, if there was a moment of ignorance being bliss, that was kind of it. Because as crushing as that was, it was only one blip on what was about to be my not-so-greatest-hits week.

But that, my friends, would be getting ahead of myself.

So let's just start with Monday morning.

I straggle through the gates, and there they are. My posse. All hanging out, waiting, checking up on me. So in that moment, in the barely rising sun they look great, even if a little bit glary.

And as I make my way over, Jimmy is the first to comment. And it isn't something about how bad he feels or anything. Nope. Monday morning's first words are, "Wow, Sid, hate to say this, but you know, you look like shit."

Fortunately this was no shocker. I had actually looked at myself in the mirror this very morning. I find it helps when I am brushing my teeth. "Yeah, thanks. I know." I look at him and sigh. "The scrabbits are back."

Imani gets the question out first. "Scrabbits?"

"Oh yeah. That's right. You wouldn't know. It was before your time. But back in the day, when I was five or six, every time 'life's pressures,'" always accompanied by an air quote, "would get beyond a certain level I would have the same dream. I was running and being chased by a jumbo scrabbit, half squirrel, half rabbit—all teeth. Not particularly pretty."

"Ew." Imani executes a nice shiver of revulsion in solidarity. "Sorry I asked."

"But on the bright side, after my third scrabbit-go-round, I got up and did some surfing, and I think, drumroll please, I may have decided on a quote for Mr. Clifton's table."

The collective reactive groans are less than heartwarming. But I shall not be deterred.

"It's attributed to Wolcott Gibbs, who used to be with *The New Yorker* magazine. And he said, or at least he supposedly said," and I open my phone so I can read it accurately, "*I wish to Christ I had your grasp of confusion.*"

Dead silence.

"Hey, come on. It's great." I look at them, sort of stunned, or maybe just stung. "I mean, 'grasp of confusion.' It's kind of so me."

Glances rapidly exchange, heads turn, smiles hide behind certain people's hands . . . Imani. And then Jimmy gives me his big brother/wannabe dad sigh. "Sid, you really need to get some sleep."

"Really? You don't like it?"

And before this can become a thing, the bell rings, and we turn to head up the stairs. I am however, not quite convinced, so I turn to Imani, who is on my left. "Really? You really think it's bad?"

Her deadpan stare is her only answer.

First the return of the scrabbit. Then the deadpan stare. Perhaps, if I were able to read tea leaves, I might have seen this as an omen, a most prophetic start to my day. If nothing else, I would have been on high alert for the rule of three.

Because yes, from there, I walk down the hall and into the science classroom where I find Mae Ann is already there, and she has managed to rearrange our seating. My usual seat is now housing Mae Lee, while the seat next to Mae Ann's is waiting to be filled. I am presuming, dreadfully, by me.

"Uh, Mae Ann." I start, and I stop. She is staring at me, expectantly, with that grin thing again plastered on her face. And you know, I don't want to hurt someone's feelings or anything, but this is not good. And I have only myself to blame.

Well, maybe I can blame Ari just a bit.

And Vikram. After all, if he didn't have this robotics challenge, none of this would have been set in motion.

Yeah, I know. I have only myself to blame. I knew better and I ignored it all because I needed her. So I used her and now she's gone off the deep end. And while a person might think this would be flattering, let me help you out here, it's not. What it *is*, is uncomfortable and creepy.

So I avoid eye contact by casually, or more accurately pathetically, complete with a faux casual veneer, looking around as I desperately try to think what to say, whereupon I catch sight of twincess number two, Mae Lee, staring at me, and with crystal clarity I now totally understand the meaning of the expression "staring daggers."

Whoa.

However, I do have a slight moment of confusion here. Is she staring daggers because I better not hurt her sister or is she staring daggers because her sister is ditching her for me? This is a fifty-fifty crapshoot question.

Either answer would not bode well for me.

But it's time. Gotta own it. Putting on my big girl pants. Because a girl's gotta do what a girl's gotta do.

And I straighten up and turn back.

"Hey, Mae Ann?" I get the grinning head spin. Ugh. "We need to talk." I head tilt toward the hallway.

Once we are there, she quirks her head and I start pacing. As much as I can't stand the twincess, this is still not an easy thing. "Look, I realize it probably seems like I might have been leading you on or something, because I asked for your help and all that, but I just want to say I think of us as friends. You know, like, friends. Like, buddies. Like, like pals."

And I pause to come up for air, but she's not saying anything. So I gulp and dive back in. "You know. I mean, I didn't mean to take advantage of your feelings or anything like that. You know. 'Cause we're friends. Right? I mean friends are just there because they're friends. Buddies."

Mae Ann is saying nothing, and I am babbling, trying to say something, but knowing nothing I say is going to make this better. And her eyes are welling. And I'm dying. And suddenly Mae Lee comes up from behind me and physically pushes me aside, sending me crashing into a locker.

"So Sid, how you feel now, lah?"

She grabs Mae Ann's hand and starts tugging her. And even I know that in whatever language it is they speak, Mae Lee is busy saying, "I told you so. I told you she is an asshole."

And right now, even though I never meant to be, from my vantage point sprawled on the floor watching them head off, I'm not sure I can argue with whatever she is saying.

But I pick myself up and set out to find them, right after I explain to Ms. Vilinsky, who of course picks now to come down the hallway, that I need to use the restroom.

The slight delay gave them all the edge they needed, meaning I have no idea where they've gone. So I manically check the hallways, then the bathrooms—and finally, with no sign of them anywhere, I mosey to the front door and just stare off down the street. Not seeing them. Not seeing anyone, really.

As I'm standing here, I feel an old, familiar presence come up beside me. For a brief second I wonder how Imani knew to come find me. Who would have told her? But then I remember this is high school and anyone could have told her because everyone already knows. She leans into my shoulder, her arm entwining itself around mine. "You okay?"

I think for a minute. Yeah. I am okay. Not happy about it, but okay with it. I knew it wasn't going to end well. At least now it is ended.

But now, since it seems like my day for risking myself, I

dive back into the deep end. "Hey 'Mani, why didn't you tell me about Ze?"

And although her arm tightens just a bit, she doesn't pull away. "I don't know exactly." Imani tilts her head onto my shoulder, and her words are slow, hesitant, and quietly personal. You know, the way a person sounds when they're figuring it out at the same time they're telling you.

"I guess because Ze was kind of still Fenny to me, right up until she," Imani catches herself again, "ze wasn't. You know we left school together when I was, I think eleven, which was still kid-dom. I mean, if you remember, it wasn't until after I transferred here that I finally got my first bra."

We break apart, laughing at the memory. I had nearly forgotten that story.

But before she derails completely, Imani dives back in. "So even though we talked and even though I knew, it was all still kind of not really real. All my Fen stories and memories are from back when ze still identified as Fenny.

"So I think, probably right up until that motorcycle pulled up and Ze jumped off, Ze really was still Fenny to me."

We stand here, looking out at the street from the front door landing, and I sense she isn't quite finished, so I wait.

"And even though I tried never to say anything, I don't know, unsupportive, I think Ze must have known even more than I did, because now we both know, ze's been in and out of New York and never reached out. If you hadn't needed a translator, I don't know; maybe I'd never have reached out either."

When Imani began speaking, I was relieved this wasn't about me. That somehow Imani didn't trust me, or something. But as she kept talking I started feeling how deeply emotional it all was for her.

"I think, maybe I was afraid of losing Fenny if I found Ze."

And we stood there, Imani's arm now re-entwined with

124

mine, staring out the window. "And I think, maybe I hurt zir."

And with that confession, I realize the need for comfort has just shifted, and it's my turn.

For the last six years, ever since we met, I learned there is one way to let her know you hear her, without pandering. Because that's mostly what we want. Just to know we told somebody and they heard us.

So without looking sideways, but with a slight push of shoulder to shoulder, I think, *Bea Arthur, wherever you are these days, I offer my apologies*, and begin, "We'll always be bosom buddies . . ." Yes. I know. It's corny . . . ."friends, sisters, and pals." Downright hokey, as a matter of fact.

But deeply meaningful.

When Imani transferred to Cooper, she discovered musical theater—and *Mame*—shortly after we met in the seventh grade. She determined then and there she was, one day, going to be Angela Lansbury, in talent, beauty, and longevity, and therefore, my job as her new BFF was to be Bea Arthur, which, I admit, I was not initially thrilled about, for many reasons. Then Mama showed me the reruns of *Maude*, and gave me some article about just how much of a force she was. After that, I have to admit, I was pretty darn happy about being Bea.

At least I was until that fateful day Imani put us down for the seventh and eighth grade talent show, or . . . lack-of-talent show.

I'm sure you can all use your imaginations with no further help from me.

I don't need to say a word. Imani knows exactly what I'm thinking, and sure enough, in spite of the slight tremor of tears I can still feel, she quietly sings the next line, "If life should reject you, there's me to protect you."

And while I'm not one hundred percent positive about that, I still melt just a bit. I mean, could anyone honestly ask for more than that?

TWENTY

I did manage to make it back to class, and Monday did, thankfully, eventually end when I collapsed in my bed, a bundle of emotions, most of which I can't even identify, but feeling overwhelmingly lost.

So I wake up groggy, and it's a fittingly gray Tuesday. I shuffle myself off to school, and there is everyone of import to me outside, apparently rather anxiously waiting for *moi*. And if you were thinking this might be welcoming, or motivating, you'd be wrong.

I immediately, somewhat suspiciously, start dragging my feet and slowing my arrival.

"Did you hear?"

The question yells its way out of Ari's mouth about four feet before my feet get there.

Now, my internal senses begin to race. They are like a frantic pack of panting dogs. No, I haven't heard anything, but should I have heard something? Now panting is ratcheting up to foaming at the mouth, and before I can calm the pack down, it's over as Imani explodes.

"The Twincesses are gone!"

I look at her, trying to understand what she just said and what "gone" means, but again, before I have a chance to get a word out, Ari is elbowing her mouth right back in the thick of it.

"Apparently . . ." Ari holds up her hand, motioning that the floor, and this story, is her exclusive.

"Long before that *Crazy Rich Asians* movie came out, Mae Lee was obsessed with this idea that she and her sister are supposed to marry into Singapore society, which is why they do that whole "lah" thing and speak that fake Chinese. So once the movie hit, talk about obsessive fan stanning."

Dramatic, emphatic pause so we may all take in her hip-stalker accusation, and now picking back up.

"So as you can imagine, when Mae Ann started crushing on our very own, do-not-call-me-Sidonie, Sid Rubin, Mae Lee saw all her planning falling apart, and she got crazier and crazier. Ergo," pause for good word usage points, "when you said—in no uncertain terms, you were definitely not going to be Mae Ann's one true pairing, Mae Lee grabbed her sister, swiped her daddy's credit card, and they flew the coop."

Ari finishes this off, beaming with the most self-satisfied of gossip-delivered afterglows, and all I can think is, *they left because I said I wouldn't be her OTP?*

Wowzerhole.

And although I still have yet to say even one word aloud, apparently I am an open source code this morning because Jimmy, of all people, stops laughing to say, "Sid? You do know they didn't leave because of you? They left because they are batshit crazy and had this planned for years. You were just a small delay factor."

"He's right, Sid." Vik chimes in. "You can't just pack up and go to another country without having made arrangements. They may be weird, and they're definitely insane . . ."

"Certifiably cray," Ari butts in, less about signifying agreement than making certain she remains in the center of this narrative.

Vik nods, but finishes his own thought. ". . . but we do know they aren't stupid."

"And honestly, Sid." Jimmy grins just enough that I know it's coming. "I know it's hard for you to believe, but you know, you just don't have that much power."

"Or allure."

"Or that certain, hmmmm, *je ne sais quoi* . . ."

Hilarious, peeps. But I do start laughing. And laughing. And gasping for air. And not exactly for the reason one might expect.

"You know the funniest part?" I say, not waiting for an answer. "All I can think about right now is I am so glad I did not say one word to my mother about Mae Ann."

And as we all head off to class, I realize I really do feel a bit lighter. And maybe that's not particularly nice, but I just can't help it. I hope they both find whatever it is they desire . . . across the ocean, far, far away.

And I mean really freaking far away! As in never coming back!

Because here, dead center, patrolling the middle of the crowded hallway, between me and my locker, obviously on the prowl, trying not to jump out of her skin is proverbial mouth-of-the-south, queen of the Cooper gossip rodeo ring, Janelle. And I had to know she was going to be here. This is way too juicy to ignore. Even my posse, my peeps, had been outside, salivating. There is no way Janelle is going to miss out.

"Ooh lah, Sid." And it's like chalk on a blackboard. The entire hallway, including my now-cringing-'cause-he-knows-what's-coming-brother, Jean, freezes and then turns anticipatorily. "Can I ask you a question?"

Having no real options, I warily proceed forward, trying to seem casual and absolutely show no fear. After all, we all know what's coming. She's done prowling. She can smell red meat. She will pounce.

"We were all just wondering, what's it like to possess a perfect record of annual incidents to be remembered by?" And the laughing begins as she turns in a circle, inviting everyone in for the kill. "This year, may I present, *The Flight of the Twins*, complete with the strapline, or subtitle for those who have yet to complete Junior English: *A Twelfth*

Year Tragicomic Tale of Two Cities. Brought to us by none other than our very own . . . Sid Rubin."

Janelle finishes with a flourish, bringing the hallway to cheers or jeers—hard to tell.

But this time I am already overtired, and ticked off just enough. I straighten up, and . . .

"Good one, Janelle."

. . . before I can say another word, Jimmy grabs my arm and steers me away. "You know, you've got to let it go. You're not going to win this one." And he stops and looks directly at me. "And Sid? Truth: it really is kind of funny."

Maybe. Maybe not.

However, I'm not ready to concede, or laugh about it, especially when Scott and I get down to the lab and realize we are left with the bulk of the coding load, plus a nasty, ugly surprise. Either Mae Ann had not been doing as much coding as she had claimed, or her parting gift was a bit of sabotage. Either way we have been duped.

Color us shook.

And peeved. And seethed.

There is, however, a silver lining to my finding a new annoyance, or perhaps more specifically rage target, which is you can let an old annoyance go. It's debilitating having too much annoyance going on at once.

Buh bye, Janelle. Hello, Mae Ann.

Sadly, neither rage nor smolder will fix any of this, so Scott and I set to work, determining it will be more efficient to recode the entire third bot rather than risk an unseen error. It will be gruesome, but does give us time to once again evaluate our theory as to how we are attacking the competition portion.

For example, just the other night, when we had two robots competing on Imani's course, it became fairly obvious one of our smarter moves would be to get sensors for each bot and add them on. Although sensors are invaluable, they are not free. Thus, while Scott and I are ensnared in this coding mess, Marcus and Ari are unavailable, out taking another fundraising meeting, while Vik is busy laying out the brochure.

Granted, we are not the only two coders in the entire school. And yes, we could have reached out to one or two, but it seemed smarter and easier at this point, with all we had done on our own bots, to backtrack and rebuild the third bot ourselves. And not to brag, but Scott and I are faster and better than anyone else here, so while another body might seem helpful, for right now, not so much.

"Hey Sid?"

We've been pretty much silently at this for about an hour I guess, when Scott's question makes me look up.

"You okay?"

And for a split second I'm confused, and then for another split second, as his meaning dawns on me, I want to scream at him to stop. To yell, *don't go there*, but I don't.

"I mean, I know it's not a lot of fun when Janelle gets going."

I nod and shrug, hoping this will suffice. While I can't disagree, I am instantly covered in incredibly awkward, so while I know he's being thoughtful, not snarky, I am absolutely not interested in talking about this. With him. It would be like Scott and I just became equals in the Janelle's Target-of-the-Day sweepstakes, which would be incredibly gross. And while I feel just a little bit bad about hating on this, I can't.

And besides, I've kind of moved on. Okay, maybe not exactly moved, but definitely inched . . . on. Forward motion am I.

Happily my one-size-fits-all shrug seems to satisfy, and we both get back to what we were doing: coding, recoding, coding, recoding.

"Hey Sid?"

Again I pause and look up, suddenly aware it's gotten

pretty late and, as I straighten up, my back is killing me. We have been in here for hours. Who knew?

"Have you decided where you want to go to school?"

My immediate thought is, *he has heard something I don't know*? "As in, am I about to be kicked out of school or something?"

Scott looks at me for a minute, totally confused. Then he laughs. "Nah. I'm sure if you survived your sixth grade hacking history, they're not getting rid of you now. I mean college. Have you picked a university?"

"No. Not yet." Which reminds me I should probably get those applications out before the folks remember to ask . . . again. "How about you?"

"I'm not sure. I'm building a database. Of everyone's choices. And I'm cross-referencing where everyone from the last three years has gone." There's a sudden hesitation in his voice. "I don't really care that much about which school I go to or where it is. I just want to be anonymous when I start. You know?"

And I look at him. And I do know. Hey, I'm as guilty of the "yuck" as the next guy. And I feel really hurt, for him . . . but not for me. Because that's when my inner light-bulb turns on and I realize Jimmy is right. My high school legacy is kind of funny. A realization that makes me want to shout.

But Scott's will never be. Which shuts me right back up.

And then I am stuck. I think maybe I should be saying something, but I don't know what it should be. Do I say I'm sorry? Do I say don't worry about it? That if we both end up going to the same school I won't tell anyone?

This is not in my comfort, nor my comforting, zone.

Which I do feel really bad about—because the sad part is I know he's just trying to make me feel better. And he's being honest and unguarded, and even vulnerable, but the truth is we weren't ever on some even playing field of

131

despair. So while he means to be generous, he really is too intimate, and now we can be uncomfortable. Or not.

Because, you know, a funny thing happened on the way to the competition. Somewhere, while I was being oblivious, I realize "Hand Jive Olney" went and became "Scott-the-Coder." And Scott-the-Coder deserves better—from me.

"Hey Scott?" I look straight at him. "I don't think you need to escape to college. I think you're gonna take it by storm."

Scott looks at me, blinks. I know he is checking for a punch line, but I really don't have one. He isn't Hand Jive anymore.

After that I don't think we say another word to each other unless it is about the code. Until eight o'clock, when Mr. Rabon knocks and gives us the signal. He is done for the night, so we are done.

And judging by the dark and empty hallways, I guess so is everyone else.

The three of us make our way out of the building and walk a block and a half over to the cross-cornered subway entrances, where we split up, each to catch our own trains.

And then it happens just as if I am living in an action movie. In one continuous shot, I take a seat, the doors close, and *boom*. From my backpack I hear a sound. No, that's not right. I hear a signal. Our group emergency ping beacon of urgency is going off.

I tear off my pack and whip out my phone. It's from Ze:

TILE-BOY SURFACED. SUNDAY IS A GO.

TWENTY-ONE

Now, as you can imagine, I am reasonably freaking out, with no place to fly my freak. It is past eight thirty on a school night, and there is no way I can "swing by Chelsea" and not be "killed by Mama."

But since we do have technology, and therefore electronic chatter, I manage to somehow "miss my stop" so I can get all the details.

Of which there are very few.

Ze did as promised: kept playing, leveling up, adding to zir inventory, and when the SwHypo went back into the cave, Ze made zir move. And with the aid of a couple of random players, managed to get back inside and grab a screen shot, which Ze kindly shares, and then translates. It is even worse looking than the first one, but it is a barely legible symbol for "yes."

And we all agree, Tile-Boy must not have gotten our initial invite on time, so he is agreeing to this coming Sunday.

Unfortunately, it is only Tuesday.

So now we will have to wait.

I make my way home pep talking to myself, wrapping my brain around believing, *hey, it's really just four more days. I mean Tuesday is really over already. Four days, no biggie. I got this.*

Well, probably not, but I've got to try something.

It already seems like an eternity since we were all on the

hunt at Ze's, but really that was only two days ago. And now, the next four days are going to take forever. And sadly I mean with a capital *F*.

What if he doesn't show? Deep breath.

I wonder if someone's made a study of this. Or at least written one of those books like, "Painful Time Tricks for the Brain" or "Time Suck for Idiots." Maybe there's an app for that.

What if he does? Calming down.

Maybe I should make one.

Who is he? Tension rising up. *Why is he?* Deeper breath.

And if for two seconds I manage to somehow forget about him, it is only because I need to code. I need to code a lot.

Make the bot go forward, make the bot go back. Deep breath. One day gone. Lift. Drop. Up. *Who?* Down. *Why?* It's way too busy in here. Breathe, Sid. Two days gone. Climb. OMG. Scaling the tower with three bots at the same time is killer. Think. We need to focus on earning the free climb. Critical if we want to win. Wait. Breathe. Wait. Think. That's it! We change from sucking the power cubes into rollers to using claws for pickup, because the rollers mean we have to take time to position the bots, time that we couldn't afford. But the risk is the claw isn't as steady a bet. Speed versus stability. Wait. We can have both. We need to program the claws to suck in the cubes. High fives. Steady under pressure. Three days gone.

Full Thorium test run late on Saturday. While the football team is away somewhere winning, Vikram works furiously with us, attaching the sensors we now have, creating the feedback loops to get them communicating, all with enough time to get Robot A onto the course minutes before Jimmy and Trey come flying in and take turns driving.

It's two perfect runs. Sensors on, timing is impressively better. Celebrations abound.

Day four is done. I race the scrabbits all night long. And now they're getting smarter. My edge is slipping.

Getting so close. All I have to do is hold on and keep it together for another few hours and meltdown will be avoided. Although the very light tap at my door that nearly forces me to jump out of my skin is not helping.

"Hey Sid?" Jean whispers from the other side.

"Yeah?"

"Can I come?"

I think no, but before I say it, I pause. He was there when we needed him. And he swore he wouldn't say anything and he hasn't. It's kind of fair. I open my door.

"Do you have to bring Aaron?"

Jean doesn't even bother to take the bait, just stares at me with that *don't be a moron* stare. I know, but I had to try. And with that, I cave.

"Yeah. Okay."

I'd love to share something sappy, like it was the start of an upturn of our sibling relationship, or having Jean with me made the remaining time bearable, but those would be, well maybe not lies, but definitely a gross exaggeration.

This time we're all here. Well other than Mae Ann, who I hope is very happy . . . in Singapore. This "we" is all our usual suspects, plus bro and Aaron, and of course, Ze. Jimmy vacates his wingman chair, allowing Vikram to join Ze in the war room closet.

They travel together and open a channel. And we all follow them into the dungeon, positioning ourselves around them, our attempt to create a kind of loose ring, so once tile-boy gets close enough, we will be preset to close in, in an effort to keep anyone else from overhearing their chat.

And right on schedule, a string of Chinese characters pop up. As the bubbles appear, Ze translates between the two.

Tile-Boy: Hello Viksation32

Viksation32: Hello.

Tile-Boy: My name is Qi, but you know me as Afexor4.

Vikram's jaw drops, and he looks over at Ze. Loud enough for all of us to hear, Vik quickly explains that in *Contagion*, Afexor4 is a legend. He'd gone ghost over a year ago; no one knows where he went, and even after he's been gone for over a year, no one can catch his status.

Tile-Boy: I have very little time, and I am very sorry I must steal your materials, but I need help and I know you are an honorable person from how you play the game.

Vik swivels to look at all of us, or at least those of us he can see from his perch within the closet, hoping we are somehow making better sense of this than he is.

I don't see anyone else's response to his confusion, but mine is an I-don't-have-a-clue shrug.

Viksation32: Help?

Tile-Boy: I am dying, and my parents will never know the truth and I cannot die without knowing someone will tell them.

With that, we forget all about maintaining a perimeter around Vik and well, Afexor4, and move to huddle in the closet doorway behind Vik and Ze.

Tile-Boy: My time is running out. I must tell you my story. I am a gaming addict. And my parents tried to stop me, but I did not listen. One day, some people came to where I was playing, tied me up, and took me to a camp for rehabilitation. But they lied to my parents. There is no rehabilitation. There is only farming. Play the game. Get the drops. They get money. Day after day. Night after night. I will soon die here, and I need someone to find my parents, to tell them the truth, and to tell them I love them and I am very sorry to have brought them shame and not to have been the son they deserved.

And as he types, we scramble to hear Ze's translation while deciding what to answer. "Ask him how we can find him? Maybe we can get someone to go get him or something?"

Tile-Boy: I cannot stay here very long. They will find me.

Vikram looks to us all helplessly. "What do we say?"

My mind is racing, trying to think of some way we can get to him. "Ask him if he can find the IP address for his computer." As I say it, my confidence grows. "If he can get it, we can trace the location of the game from our end." Ze types, and I keep verbally processing. "If he's really part of a farming operation, the real question will be whether or not it's hidden behind a VPN, in which case it will be a lot more complicated, and," now even Ze pauses to stare over with a *shut up* on zir lips. "Never mind. Let's just hope he can get it and we can trace it."

Ze types.

Tile-Boy responds: I cannot risk looking.

Group stomach drop. Everyone turns back to me. And just as I'm about to get defensive and say something like "I'm not a miracle worker," I realize maybe I am. Well, not a miracle worker, but a woman with a plan.

I duck out of the closet and grab my phone, frantically trying to DM @SpitPolishGames and praying Dan-the-heretofore-useless-wonder is there. I type. And miracle of miracles, he answers.

"Got it." As I scream, the closet door, jammed with everyone watching, parts like the proverbial Red Sea, giving me a direct eye-line to Ze. "Tell him," I slow down to read the message word for word, "to just type /debug:IP into his chat window to get the current IP of his computer."

Ze types. And we wait. And there it is. An electronic lifeline. Between Qi and us.

TWENTY-TWO

By four o'clock, we are racing around the corner. And then another until we burst through the double doors, grinding to a stop to have our bags scanned, which given the amount of electronic toys between us all, takes an annoying amount of time.

As we get through, I realize it's pretty quiet inside, because, duh, it is Sunday. My emotional roller coaster starts slowly making its way over the edge, preparing for its next drop, which looms directly ahead . . .

. . . at the elevated desk sergeant's desk. The desk sergeant being the only incredibly busy party, with one not-quite-firing-on-all-cylinders would-be client. Happily the sergeant not only looks up but recognizes us, and ignoring the cacophony emanating from the man ahead of us, laughs, although not particularly kindly, and says, "Oh yeah, he's back there. Just go right on through."

Which is great for three reasons. One, it's Sunday and he's here. Two, time is of the essence. And three, if I don't need to be in the waiting area, which I can confirm shows no sign of having been cleaned since my last visit, my ever so slightly germaphobic self has no reason to appear.

My roller coaster is back on the rise as we take off, tearing around the corner, until we are bursting in on our old pal—no, that might be too much of an exaggeration, bursting into Detective Robert Tsarnowsky's office—where we throw the door open, crashing it head on into some guy.

138

Ow.

"Nice work, Sid." Tsarnowsky seems much more amused than perturbed. "Maybe you broke his nose. I keep telling him he needs to get it fixed. Broke it in a couple of places back in his soccer days, but he was too busy heading balls or something to get it fixed properly."

And despite his partner's glare and our obvious need to talk, Tsarno the Barno, as I like to think of him, is too busy amusing himself to let us interrupt.

"You know, with your aim, you might think about trying out for the football team. Put that uncanny talent to use."

Hysterical, Barno. Guffaw. Guffaw. Must be nice to find yourself so amusing.

"Let me introduce you to your latest target." Tsarnowsky continues unabated. "Officer DeShawn Jordan." We look over, nod, and we're done. But he's not. "DeShawn, let me introduce you to infamous-in-these-parts, dangerous-to-stand-next-to, or under, Sidonie Rubin, and her gang of LARPers. Let's see, we have Jimmy, hmmm, Vikram, Ari, and Imani, right?

"And," Tsarno spots Ze. "Who's this?"

I interrupt, or at least talk over this introduction to clarify my name is Sid, before Tsarno even finishes his question. I do, however, manage to finish said interrupting in time to answer his question.

"This is Ze. Ze is helping us with a case."

I am pleased to report Tsarno did not even blink. About the Ze of it all. But referring to our case, he did more than blink. He bugged out his eyes, snorted a bit, and even did that drawn-out-fake-surprise-sarcastic thing.

"Wow. You have a case? You don't say."

"Hysterical." And I wait for him to put his eyeballs away. "No. What I mean," and pause to correct myself here. "What we mean is *you* have a case. And it's urgent. And you need to jump all over it, or whatever it is you do, before someone dies."

Tsarno pauses, surveys all of us, and gets our urgency, because he glances at DeShawn, nods, and we fill them in.

"So just so I'm getting all this correctly." Tsarnowsky pauses and looks back down to his notes. "You," and he looks over to Vikram, "you were playing some internet game called *Contagion*. And your," and again he scans his notes, "inventory was stolen by some guy named Qi who is purportedly being held hostage somewhere in China, and who you think is about to die." He looks at us, to put it kindly, slightly askance. "And you know all this because this one here," head motioning towards Ze, "translated a mah-jongg tile."

Which I have to admit, when put that way, sounds a tad improbable, and a lot far-fetched. Of course, the barely disguised scoffing isn't helping either.

"Look, Detective." Vikram stands up. "I know this sounds very foolish and dramatic, but it's not."

"He's right." Jimmy chimes in. "This is not just because Ze translated a tile. Sid had Qi go find his IP address, so we could trace it and determine first if he is actually in China, and not some guy around the corner spoofing us, and then, if he was who he said he was, we could use the trace to try and save him."

Getting his metaphorical arm into it, he verbally tosses a tight spiral right into Tsarno's hands. "You do remember, Detective, Sid's pretty good with this stuff."

Which does seem to hit home. As Tsarnowsky stares hard at me, I meet his eyes and make one final plea.

"You must know someone who can do something. You know, run a check on it. I mean if they would just go over there and find out it's nothing, then we'd all know we were suckered. Which would make no sense, but there you have it."

Tsarno stares at me, evaluating. I sit, staring back, hoping whatever my stare says is the right answer.

"So DeShawn, do we know anyone who can just dash over to," and again Tsarnowsky looks down at his notes,

"Anhui Province, in China, and just," pause for emphasis of our idiocracy, "check this out?"

Apparently my stare came up short. We know we're being mocked and there's not a damn thing we can do about it, except collect ourselves and our things and head to the door. Unless . . .

"Look." I wheel back around. "We came here because I thought you would listen. Ze," I point to my left, "thought we should put out an SOS on a forum to reach all gamers in the province. See if we can use our recovered geolocation to get them to group together to find this place, crash wherever or whatever it is, and rescue Qi."

I sense Tsarnowsky is growing uneasy. Although he may not be a web expert, he knows what I just said is not out of the question. I'm not sure it would actually work, but it sounds pretty good as a spur-of-the-moment backup plan. I watch as he and Officer Jordan exchange glances. Then I press on.

"But thanks anyway."

DeShawn looks at Tsarnowsky. "I can give Bobby Hong a call. He works in the Chinatown division. Maybe they know someone."

Tsarnowsky nods. DeShawn leaves. We inch our way back in. But remember, no one likes to be played.

"So, any of your parents know you were dropping by today?"

The shifting eyes and shuffling feet speak volumes.

"I'll take that as a *no*. Hard to believe you haven't managed to share your latest hijinks with them."

Now we all know, I do love a great word choice. Not to mention a bit of a dare. And maybe even a bit of a distraction. "Did you know hijinks actually comes from a Scottish drinking game?"

And with that Tsarnowsky gives me the most curious of looks, which I choose to interpret as, "gosh I've missed you," laughs, and leans back in his chair. "No, Sid, I did not."

"Well, the game doesn't seem to have any known strategy or anything, but apparently it did involve dice."

"Of course."

Yeah. I am right. That is definitely an "I've missed you." And the tension breaks for at least the moment.

Officer Jordan returns with some not-bad news. He's reached Detective Hong, who it turns out is at least familiar with what we were talking about, if not the specifics. So Detective Hong has agreed to reach out to a police officer he knows in China and see what they might have to say.

And with that we are sent on our way with a promise they will follow up and let us know.

I have to say Tsarnowsky did get in the last digs in of the day. We were in the hallway, heading out, and he, let's not say yells, but announces, "Don't forget, when I have news, I will need to find you. Hate to shock your parents a second time."

Checkmate.

So while I didn't relish doing it, I went home and told the parents our agreed-upon CliffsNotes version of events, about Vikram being ripped off, and how we all met up to play the game and find the thief, as though it was something that had happened overnight. I am relieved to report it didn't go too poorly.

I don't want to say it went great, either.

But with no actual wrongdoing—all we did was chat with some dude in the game who put up a tile saying SOS in Chinese, and we went to the police—we left our parents nothing to hang us, or ground us, for. So other than a slightly raised eyebrow or two, I am goodish to go.

But I know thin ice when I am skating on it. And thus I head directly upstairs whereupon I force myself to finish my English paper.

Monday and Tuesday pass pretty uneventfully. By that I mean no word. By Wednesday afternoon, we have tested all the robots, and it is time for bag and tag, which means our time for building robots is up, and ready or not, they are locked away until the competition begins.

Thursday. Yeah, it's now Thursday and eerily quiet. I want to call Tsarno, but I don't. I know if he had something to tell us, he would. Well, not exactly true. In all truthfulness, I would have called him, but we took a vote and agreed we would not check in before Tuesday of next week.

So here I am, on the losing side, sulking, but not calling. Which I'm sure is not a big surprise. But I didn't think it would be four to one. Against me.

Finally the call did come. Right after he called our parents *first*, which was incredibly annoying, insulting, and, I'm going to concede, most likely mandated protocol.

I like to think our history deserves better than simple spite.

TWENTY-THREE

We are all gathered in a cinder-block conference room with one of those big speakerphone things in the middle of the table and a monitor at the far end. Along with Ze and Jean, my parents, Imani's parents, and Vik's Dad are also in attendance.

Apparently, since Aaron was not with us at the police station, I am rather pleased to report he is keeping himself anonymous, or at least his parents uncontacted, and I can't say as I blame him.

After a few minutes, the door opens, and in come Detective Tsarnowsky, along with Officer Jordan and Lieutenant Raymond P. Clark, who is making the rounds, shaking hands with everyone in the room. When he gets to me, he pauses and smiles. "It's good to see you again, Sidonie." And with that, he motions to us to sit.

"I want to thank you all for coming down here this evening, and I'd like to introduce you all to Detective Hong."

A very well dressed, very fit Asian man, maybe thirty or so, walks into the room, carrying a folder, broadly smiling as he makes his way toward the monitor. "Bobby, please. Only my mother calls me Detective Hong." And as everyone chuckles and relaxes just a bit, he takes a minute to open the folder and place it on the table, although he doesn't take a seat.

"I'd like to thank Detective Tsarnowsky and Officer DeShawn Jordan for reaching out to me. And I'd like to apologize to all of you about the hour, but it is now eight o'clock in the morning *tomorrow* in Hefei, China. In addition, I'd like to thank Vikram. Where are you?" He pauses, waiting for a sign, and as Vikram raises his hand, "Jimmy?" As Jimmy's hand goes up, Bobby continues until we have all been identified.

"When Officer Jordan phoned me, your story had just enough whisper of truth, I felt I needed to check with a colleague. In Chinese, there is an old proverb I learned from my grandparents, which I had more or less forgotten. It is: 有缘千里来相会 *yǒu yuán qiān lǐ lái xiāng huì.* It means fate brings people together no matter how far apart they may be. Something about DeShawn's call made me remember that saying.

"So I called Senior Superintendent Wang, an officer I knew from a joint task force, and asked if she could somehow do a quick check of your story, the address, whatever was possible." Here Bobby pauses to flip a few pieces of paper in his folder until he finds the one he wants, which he picks up and proceeds to read from directly.

"Yesterday, at five o'clock in the morning, Hefei time, a raid was conducted on an internet addiction camp in Anhui Province. Six people were arrested on the spot, one hundred and eight addicts are being evaluated for further treatment or possible release, and seven were rushed to hospitals, including your friend Qi."

As he puts the paper back, he smiles at all of us. "You are all heroes. You saved the lives of seven people."

Chills run up my spine, and part of me wants to scream and part of me wants to cry. Some of it is pure relief and joy because if we hadn't been heard, if I wasn't validated, it would have been too late. I desperately wish I could step out into the hallway alone and just hug myself for a minute.

I must have missed something being said, because all of a sudden the remote is clicked and a dark-haired, serious-looking woman appears on the monitor.

Bobby Hong is saying, "Hello. Can you hear us okay?" At her nod, he turns back to the table.

"Everyone, I would like to introduce my colleague, Senior Superintendent Wang." And with that, Bobby pulls a chair up next to the monitor, facing us, but turned in slightly, so he can also keep an eye on the screen.

"Thank you, Detective Hong." And if "Bobby" is all warm and fuzzy, Senior Superintendent Wang is all business. She sits perfectly straight, but her eyes travel until she makes contact with each of us.

When she resumes speaking, you get the sense no words are wasted. "We want to say thank you to all of you for your assistance in closing down what we discovered was a fairly small but still very sophisticated criminal operation. Our investigation shows the rehabilitation school was legitimate, but it was for a wealthy clientele only, and a front for the rest of the operation." Senior Superintendent Wang waits, letting us absorb her words.

I don't know what anyone else's reactions are, because I am hanging on her every word.

"In 2008, China became the first nation to declare internet addiction a clinical disorder, which is a great and forward-thinking initiative." Wang's English is impeccable, deliberate. "But as with all great positive thinking, there are some people who see negative opportunity.

"What we now know is they used two scouts. These were men whose job it was to go from gaming den to gaming den, watching the competition, ranking not only the players, but also their addiction levels. If you were to think of them perhaps as music or, even better, basketball scouts, they would go to a game, spot the talent, check out their backgrounds, and if everything hit their checklist, they would then, and only then, begin recruiting them."

Here, Wang allows a brief pause before she continues, "Which means recruiting their parents. Once a target was identified, they would seek out those who had mothers,

146

fathers, or any relatives who were without means, desperate, a little bit less sophisticated, living in provinces far away, and woo them with promises of success and pictures from the legitimate side of the business.

"There are now an estimated twenty-three million Chinese people suffering with gaming addiction."

The gasp from our group was surprisingly audible, and Wang's smile surprisingly gentle. "You must remember, we are over seven hundred *million* computer users."

With each word that Senior Superintendent Wang speaks, the size and the scope has me mesmerized and feeling a combination of awe while feeling smaller, and thankful I didn't know any of this. We were all just playing a game.

"And like all addicts, nothing will keep them from their next fix. This is why some people call gaming 'electronic heroin.'

"So when this savior appears, the parents voluntarily, even *thankfully*, sign the papers giving over control of their children to this center, not knowing they are unwittingly signing their child's death certificate. This very select group of young people will, instead of being treated, become what are called 'gold farmers.' They will have their addictions fed, playing hour after hour, mining the farm for drop after drop, lost in the haze, until they tragically choke on their own games and die.

"And if, like the young man, Qi, they prove to have more stamina than anticipated, it is of no consequence, because the parents have been already informed that 'despite their best efforts, their son was too far gone' and had passed away in his sleep.

"So they have created a loop, an unlimited supply of game-addicts to choose from, who become farmers to fulfill market demand as they see fit."

I hear Mama's *"merde"* slice through the silence. It's as good a summary as any. Wow.

147

For the first time, Officer Wang leans slightly back. She becomes just a bit less formal, more conversational as she asks, "And why gold farming? I suppose the simple answer is because they can. There was a time, here in China, these were huge operations, but as the games became savvier, and many of them began to allow players to resell inside their own systems, many of them moved on to other lucrative schemes, and of course other 'opportunities' arose in disinformation and such.

"But for a very small number of entrepreneurs willing to bide their time, it was perfect. They set about building community and government respect using their addiction treatment centers, which provided them an influx of legitimate children. And if one of the children dies, which sadly some do, because some are too far gone to save, the community grieves for those poor people who are working so hard to fight this deadly scourge. Must be so tough to see.

"And while the good people weep for their loss, and hail them as heroes, our two-faced thieves hide all their earnings in cryptocurrencies, with no paper trail of illicit money for the Chinese government to follow. Even the deposits are hidden by a VPN."

And she gives us a rueful kind of smile. "I believe the American expression is they are crying all the way to the bank."

And almost as though she has shown us too much, Senior Superintendent Wang sits back up and continues perfunctorily, "We believe there were six people involved in this operation, the two scouts, the two business owners, and two guards, all of whom have been arrested.

"We also believe there was one additional person, a Chinese national, the brother-in-law of one of the guards, who is now living in Canada. It appears his job was solely to get the cryptocurrency and transfer its digital wallet into hard cash or other assets, for which he was paid a fee. At this

148

time we are not sure he knew anything about the actual source of the money."

We hear a knock coming from behind Wang, followed by a bit of commotion, which causes her to pause, and gives us a chance to exchange looks. I now know what incredulous looks like when it isn't faked. That would be the parent row.

As for us, we just look like, well, pardon the English, holy shit.

Then Wang is back. "Every rescue story needs a miracle. The Anhui boys' miracle might be that somehow, even though these ruthless men used the VPN for their financial transactions, they did not for their farming. It was a careless mistake. If they had, your IP idea would not have been so simple, and we would most likely not be here today."

"But this is why, as Detective Hong alluded, you have exceptional *yuánfèn* 緣分, which is a Chinese concept, a fateful coincidence, perhaps most similar to karma. Out of seven and a half billion people, you were destined for each other."

And with that, Senior Superintendent Wang smiles and bows her head. Her portion is finished.

Or not. Because before we can say anything, Bobby Hong stands back up.

"Senior Superintendent Wang and I have one more item. Qi would like to speak to you. But please remember, although his doctors say thanks to you he will survive, he is very weak. And his appearance is very sad. But he will be okay. It will just take time."

With that, Wang turns the camera around, and there, in a hospital bed propped up with pillows, is the skinniest man I've ever seen . . . at least alive. He looks like one of the photos of Holocaust survivors, or maybe from the AIDS epidemic.

As he begins speaking, Wang begins to translate, but stops as she hears Ze softly doing the same.

149

"Hello Viksation32. I wish to say I am sorry for the trouble I have caused for you, but I thank you for saving my life."

"Hello Qi." Vik stands up with a small wave. "We are very happy to see you alive."

"Thank you. I believed you would come."

Which was the opening we were all waiting for. And we didn't need to prompt Vik. He was all over it. "Why?"

"I am not sure. But I think because, when you don't know whom to trust, you must think deeply on who you know. And I know you. For many years now. You play smart, but you always play fair."

Qi shifts slightly, trying to leverage up a bit on his pillow. "Xiong and I were taken together, in the same car, and over time we learned to leave messages for each other in the game we were farming. So one day I know he is dying and I must try to save him. And I must save me. And so I think back to playing *Contagion* and I think, if I can get back to there, I will maybe find somebody who will understand."

Ze is completely transfixed, even as ze continues to translate. "And so I stole your items. It was not honorable, but I was desperate." Qi attempts a smile as he says, "I hoped you would be insulted enough to come and find me."

"Okay, but why didn't you just ask?"

And although Qi answers, Ze's translation isn't immediately there. And when I look over, I am stunned to see tears running down Ze's cheek. Slowly ze picks back up. "Because I could not risk contact with anyone else. I know," and once again, Ze's voice cracks. Then ze takes a small break followed by a deep breath, pulling it back together. Ze finishes: "I am a disappointment to my family, but I did not want to die. So I believe you will come. And I am right."

And as Vikram answers, I realize I now have some of my Ze questions answered too. Why ze is in New York City

150

alone. Why ze never reached out. I risk a glance at Imani, who is looking at me, a tear running down her cheek. Yeah, those answers hurt.

"You are only partly right." Vikram walks over to where I am sitting. "We all came, but not because of me. None of us would have come without Sid. She was much more determined to avenge my loss than I was."

And all of a sudden, it was all eyes on me. Talk about an ungainly fluster of blush. But I manage to smile and say, *"Faut pas toucher mes amis."*

Fortunately, I know Ze knows French.

TWENTY-FOUR

And there was a bit more, something about Qi being a "bare branch," which is apparently a low-income, low-status man who is typically unmarriageable, so they become the endpoint for a family tree. In China, there are 117 boys for every 100 girls. So not every boy will have a chance to meet a girl to marry.

Then there was news of Qi's pal, Xiong, who was the motivation for all of this. He was alive when they got there, but barely. He is now in a coma and may not survive.

And then when everyone had finished, Senior Superintendent Wang presented us with letters of appreciation from the Chinese government, copies of which Bobby distributed, all grins and winks, while the originals are being sent. Detective Tsarnowsky then presented us certificates of recognition from the New York Police Department, both of which will look great on those college apps, but of more immediate importance, they are like "get out of parental jail free" proclamations.

And don't think Tsarno doesn't know it. When we got to mine, he leaned over very quietly and said, "I think this means you might owe me one someday."

We both laughed.

So now, I'd love to tell you we are all flying high and feeling heroic, or at least vindicated, but the reality is far different. The truth is we are all feeling emotionally overwhelmed, maybe even a bit despondent. The anticlimax of this one is tough.

Ze came by school during lunch, to tell us ze's returning home to China. Seeing our parents in the room that night, especially Imani's, and then Qi's parents huddling in the background, unleashed a need for zir.

I don't ask, but I really hope Xing isn't going with Ze. There's no real reason, except Xing gives me the heebie-jee-bies. And I don't like the heebie-jeebies. Feel free to extrapolate.

And with no robots to code and no world to save, I am a bit lost, so I join Imani's crew in taking down "the set," trying to find a sense of normalcy or at least a way to keep busy. I'm under the stage, stacking old flats, saving them for another day. Which won't be mine. Because I will have moved on.

Melancholy anyone?

And as I finish tucking the flat upright, I see the gang coming to find me. "Hey."

"Hey." Vikram pushes slightly ahead. "We all wanted to say thank you because we know we never would have found Qi if you weren't so . . ."

And as Vik pauses to choose his best option, Jimmy sees the opening and jumps in with, "Dog with a bone." Which he accompanies with a wink.

And apparently that's not all, folks. Step right up and give the wheel a spin. We are playing apology-go-round.

Next up is Ari. "Yeah, I know. I also want to say I'm sorry. I know I sort of pushed the whole Mae Ann thing, but wow, I truly had no idea. I just knew she had this crush on you and I thought, hey, why not? Maybe it would be fun. I mean we all knew she was a bit nutty; we just didn't know she was cray cray . . . cra-ay!"

And see, just like I said, cat paw/lick!

Imani rolls her eyes and pushes forward, carrying a

package. "Ari is now, and forever, out of the matchmaking business, and since all of us have a hundred reasons to feel bad, we all chipped in and got you a present."

I'm really stunned. And touched. And I take the wrapped package and open it to find a hardcover copy of *Princess Princess Ever After* by Katie O'Neill. As my hands pet the glossiness, a tactile, sensory delight, I hear Ari say, "It's a first edition."

I gently flip the pages, and knew I was wrong. I wasn't really stunned two seconds ago, because now I am really, truly stunned. There, in the middle, is a ticket to Comic Con. I look up at my friends, each of them grinning super big and wearing a matching ticket, dangling from around their necks.

It's almost as if I have been dropped into another world. I become a third person to myself, as I realize Sid the Word-ster is struck dumb. She opens her mouth several times, but she has no idea what to say.

Finally, I close my mouth, take out my matching ticket, hug the book to my chest, and just smile. The gift is perfect. No. That's not it. The gift is fabulous and wonderful and just right. But what is perfect, in this moment, is everything ... especially my friends.

TWENTY-FIVE

And we're finally here. Welcome to *FIRST* Power Up. It's the qualifiers, and it's insane. Sixty-something teams are gathering together from all over New York and a couple of neighboring states to compete for the next two days.

I make my way into the schoolyard, which has been transformed by hanging banners for every school. I head up to the front door, which is harder than it sounds as I am literally being "lovingly greeted" by members of our spirit team at every turn. It seems Janelle has them out in full force, welcoming every competitor with, "Thoriums thank you for this honor of competition."

And even though it strikes me as a bit street corner accost-ish, as opposed to graciously professional, I have to admit it seems to be going over really well. But then again, everyone is so incredibly psyched to be here, I think everything is pretty high on the happy-making scale right now.

Janelle sees me swerving to avoid a group of cheering crosstown rivals, nearly taking out an unsuspecting greeter on my left. She laughs, blows a playful kiss across the yard. I air catch it in my fist and double tap my heart before heading in the main doors into even more madness.

See? Lighthearted. High spirits. Antics everywhere. Even me.

Teams, coaches, parents, guests, and more or less the entire world are making their way toward the gymnasium, with groups stopping to hold last-minute meetings, organize signs, and whatever else all the whispers, shouts, giggles, and occasional tears mean.

As I watch a young girl racing to the bathroom, followed worriedly by, I am guessing, a coach, I realize how far I've come. Freshman year, I will acknowledge that might have been me.

If I thought the hallway was busy, the cacophony as I enter the gym is one wall of sound. I take a minute to let my ears adjust, spot my parents, who are in their predetermined seats, sitting with Imani, Vik and Jimmy's folks, of course. Pause for a quick wave. And then, keep moving.

Slowly.

We are one incredibly raucous, jumbo party, with many appendages flying every which what way, and no matter which what way I move, I am still caught in that whole swimming upstream thing. Through the River of Nerds. Duck. Into the Deluge of Geeks. Dodge. Upstream through a Swarm of Trekkies, which is so totally cool. Vulcan salute. Sidestep. Stop for air. And start all over.

But everyone is laughing, "pardon-ing," "scusing." I keep treading and finally manage to snake my way through to Thorium-land, located right at the arena's edge, with most of my toes intact.

My last few feet are easy as Marcus sees me, and bam, smiles wide and sexy, which is the cue for other people to turn and see why he is smiling, and lo and behold the crowd makes way for me. Well, really for him. Dang.

I see Vik and Ari are already here, and, yep, here come Jimmy, Imani, and Trey shouldering through from the other side.

The clock has already begun a formal countdown. As the hosting school, we are scheduled to be first up.

Question: why is it all school mics come with screeching feedback?

Answer: to signal in the most despicable, painful way

156

possible we are to not only be ready for, but pay attention to, the welcoming remarks.

Which are interrupted constantly by the usual generic appropriate applause, mostly from parents and teachers, but in addition, all these random spirit cheers keep popping up, and now someone has gone and launched a jumbo balloon, which is being batted throughout the bleachers.

Thoriums, at least the playing squad, have no time for such merriment. We are quietly huddling, reviewing last-minute notes and finalizing, one last time, our strategy.

Which did get kind of tricky at one point. Each drive team has five people, one of whom is a technician. Each team has three drive teams. As you can guess, we were left short one technician. Gone to Singapore. Lah.

Dee. Dah.

I picked Jean.

Which really wasn't all that hard for me. He really is good. Not as good as me, but hey. So few are. I know, sometimes amusing myself is way too much fun.

But as rarely happens, in this case my choice is good for the school, too. It is weird to realize it and for a moment kind of sad, but none of us will be here next year to participate. We will all be dreaded freshmen again at some university somewhere. Leaving a proven legacy player will help next year's bumper crop of Smither's Suckers, as even now, I already like to think of them.

So we are all good, right up until it gets tricky again. Only this time, it was kind of my fault. Well, not really. Vik and Marcus were taking two of the "coach" positions, and Smitty was going to be the third. And then they came to me. To tell me they wanted me to be the third. Which blew me away. I was honestly shocked. But I did say yes.

So now Jean is my technician. Because their suggested replacement nominee was Aaron . . . and to that I did say no. In no uncertain terms. Slurp.

Yes. That was mean. But I don't feel all that bad.

And now, deep breath, we are sorted and it is "go" time. Marcus gives one last "Thoriums Rule" rah. We step forward for our first-round challenge, and I know I am ready. I look at Jean, fist bump, "We have so got this."

It's game on.

And as we start and the surface lights up, I feel the smile growing on my face. We cross the auto-line perfectly, drivers take over, and I am ecstatic, elated, and truly *mostly* thrillieved.

Back when Scott and I were recoding, we got into a rip-roaring argument that went on for a couple of days. I believed our best approach to the course was going to be to take no approach. My thinking was most teams are going to look at the course and say "we're blue; remember we need to start on the left." Which is exactly where we had been when we started.

I put up a huge fight to code what felt counterintuitive, no left/no right, but rather code the bot to go down the middle and we determine it from there.

We did finally agree, or I just wore him out, and we recoded, with the gamble that we will shoot dead center and trust the quickness of Jimmy's reflexes to claim the scale one touch faster. A huge payoff if we're right.

And now we are here. The moment of truth. Will the move I know appears to be the slower one actually be the quicker move because we won't have to override a commitment based on where the scale falls?

It's been so long since we bagged and tagged our equipment and, I don't know, chased a kidnapper across the globe, I forgot how much I had riding on this opening.

Auto mode switches to driver control. Jimmy moves and . . . slam dunk!

We've got control of the switches. And the scale. And now our third bot, slower on speed but built to corner, is loading a cube and heading to the vault.

Where we agreed, this time without a fight, not to

worry about anything other than first filling the Levitate column. That option buys us one free robot climb up the scale at the end, and that's our first aim. After that, we check where we have held ownership best, either the scale or the switches, and then attempt to fill that boost column accordingly.

And as I'm watching Marcus deliver a power-up cube through the portal exchange, my eye catches sight of my competitor in the alliance station next to it. She has dark hair and greenish eyes, and all of a sudden her hands are flying to emphasize something as she tells a slim, dark-haired young man next to her something.

And yes. I am a smitten kitten.

One who is jolted out of a staring, gaping daze by a burst of screaming, jumping, and hugging. Scott's flashing me a thumbs up sign. Jimmy and Marcus are chest bumping. And I look up to realize we have three robots dangling from the scale. Vik and Ari grab me in a big hug. And from over a shoulder, in case I hadn't put two and two together yet, the final scoreboard tells me we have won our first round.

Was it all a blur or a blank? Hard to say. Let's just go with, I don't exactly remember all the details.

However, as I squeeze out of the hug sandwich, I do suddenly remember with stunning clarity how a large part of participating in *FIRST* Robotics is being a Gracious Professional.

I should do that.

So while the gang starts to exit our station, heading to the left, making way for the next team up, I head right. And even though I know I'm being watched, I don't stop. I slip away from Thorium-land and make my way over to the other side, until I find my competitor, standing with the same guy she was arguing with when I spotted her in their Alliance Station.

"Hey." I walk right on up and smile. "Ummmm, you guys were really great."

And the closer I get, the more amazing her eyes are. They're actually a very pure, very pale green color, which I can see quite clearly because they are closely watching me, even as she says nothing.

So now I have two choices, one of which is to fake some kind of smile, turn and make like a banana and split, which presumably would have the added bonus of lessening the pounding of my pulse in my jaw. But I ignore option one and go for the second choice, adjusting my glasses and doing something I have never done.

"My name's Sid. And I was wondering if you wanted to go get something to eat. I mean maybe later. I know we still have races to do and stuff."

And as I finish, she gives me a look I'm not sure how to interpret, abruptly turns to the guy who is still there, and as her hands start moving, I realize she's signing. And whatever she is signing has grown into a rather animated back and forth, until finally the guy rolls his eyes and turns to me.

"My name is Joe." And as he speaks, I am listening closely because I realize that he, too, is deaf, and he has the slightly high-pitched tone of someone who speaks from their throat and not their diaphragm. "And she says to tell you to come back when you can ask her directly."

And with that, Joe shrugs, looks back to the girl and gestures the you-don't-have-to-be-deaf-to-get-it splayed-hands shrug, meaning, "happy now?"

And with that, they both turn and start walking away.

And I shout after them, "Tell her we have a date," only to realize that's probably not my best move. It is, however, a perfectly proper example of something falling on deaf ears. Which is probably not funny to a deaf person. But maybe it is. I honestly don't know.

And I stand here, scanning the crowd, which has swallowed them up, for about thirty seconds while I debate whether or not I should be feeling deflated, but nah. I think, you know what? I think I am feeling—challenged.

And I, Sid the Kid, I am up for this. I accept this challenge. I *will* find her. And when I do, I *will* ask her myself.

Turn on heel. Walk away. Add a little swagger.

Got to go get started with a plan.

And then pause. 'Cause you know what I'm thinking? This would be easier if I'd gotten her name. And then unpause. Because you know what? I'm not worried. If I can find some random dude in Anhui Province, I got this.

ACKNOWLEDGMENTS

There are many people to whom I am indebted for their help, their support, and their incredible kindnesses along the way.

To readers, librarians, booksellers, bloggers, reviewers, dear friends, and fellow authors, who have embraced "Sid," and by extension, me, please know, your hugs are everything.

Tom Carbone, a man who for some reason answered an email with a subject line of "help," I will always be grateful. Without you, Sid's gaming would have no Veritas, nor Gravitas— neither truth nor dignity. Thank you, Tom, for leveling me up, and then some.

Taycora Canfield, who took my call and intro- duced me to both Robotics and the amazing students who comprise Team 79 KRUNCH. Thank you, Coach Canfield. And thank you Kelley Hays. And thank you East Lake High School students Kayley Brkljacic, Carter Dabney, Jack Daniels, Allie Ghisson, Alex Iannucci, Aaron Lang, Orion Mendes, Alex Pelletier, Joe Sanders, Canada Tibbatts, and Austin Viens- DeRuisseau for a most amazing afternoon. Your commitment and enthusiasm took this story unexpected places.

FIRST® INSPIRES. Dean Kamen and Dr. Woodie Flowers, what an amazing organization you have built. I was thrilled to "borrow" a small part of it. Haley Dunn and Amanda Bessette, thank you for making that possible and real. Thank you all for inspiring so many to achieve brainy rock stardom.

Fay Jacobs. More than a wordsmith par excellence, you are an adept translator of gibberish, a reader of writer's tongue, and a soother of writer's nerves. And you are my friend. Thank You.

Russell Kolody, for always "riding shotgun" when I need it, thank you.

Shamim Sarif and Hanan Kattan, "Annie" adores you. Alex Kelm, it was a most surprising and helpful conversation, thank you. Pat Heil. Scrabbits. Just perfect. To Ellen Burditt and Joe Saraceni, thank you for the backstopping. Ann Aptaker, Jesikah Sundin, Amanda June Hagarty, Sheryl Wright, Gregory Murphy, Michael Boyle, Brenda Abell… it truly does take a village, thank you.

Cheryl Head. Thank you for the phone support. Rachel Talalay. Thank you for saying Sid is "that kind of cool."

Ann McMan. Your cover art leaves me striving to write "worthy."

Bywater Books. My Publisher. Thank you all for believing in me and loving "Sid." Salem West, Marianne K. Martin—you make the world a better place. Elizabeth Andersen and Nancy Squires, my copy editing and proofreading pals, you make it easier to understand. ☺

For friends, who take that extra minute to ask how it's going.

And for family, who doesn't, because they already know.

And for Nancy Prescott, my partner, who knows, but asks anyway.

She makes this journey possible.

I love you all.

ABOUT THE AUTHOR

Stefani Deoul is the author of the Sid Rubin Silicon Alley Adventures, a young adult mystery series. The first book in the series, *On a LARP* is a multiple award winner, including an Independent Publisher's Award (IPPY) for Multicultural Fiction—Juvenile/Young Adult. Stefani's debut novel was the award-winning, women's literary fiction, *The Carousel*. As a television producer her resume includes an array of series such as *Haven* for the SyFy Network, *The Dead Zone*, *Dresden Files* and *Missing*.

Along with producing five seasons of *Haven*, based on the Stephen King story *The Colorado Kid*, Stefani finally succumbed to the allure of acting, "starring" as the off camera, and uncredited, radio dispatcher, Laverne.

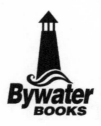

Bywater
BOOKS

At Bywater Books we love good books about lesbians just like you do, and we're committed to bringing the best of contemporary lesbian writing to our avid readers. Our editorial team is dedicated to finding and developing outstanding writers who create books you won't want to put down.

We sponsor the Bywater Prize for Fiction to help with this quest. Each prizewinner receives $1,000 and publication of their novel. We have already discovered amazing writers like Jill Malone, Sally Bellerose, and Hilary Sloin through the Bywater Prize. Which exciting new writer will we find next?

For more information about Bywater Books and the annual Bywater Prize for Fiction, please visit our website.

www.bywaterbooks.com